12 DAYS

New Creation Transformations

12 DAYS

New Creation Transformations

By
Jude Mogyordy

TATE PUBLISHING
AND ENTERPRISES, LLC

DEDICATION

To my parents, Paul and Betty, who set the standard of integrity and character in my life.

To Ann Trousdale, who brought me the message of grace and who nurtured and discipled me in those first years.

To all the pastors of my heart—

Father Babituz who taught me that Jesus loves us all unconditionally.

Rev. Ray Shear who brought healing and freedom to my captive heart.

Rev. Reid Doster who challenged me to be a part of a corporate body.

Rev. Jerry Claunch who made church real and relevant and rich.

Rev. Rick Amato who honored me and promoted me in the body.

Rev. Rodney Howard-Browne who brought true revival, new vision and joy unspeakable to me.

Rev. Christian Harfouche who put words to the new creation I have become.

"Mama Hugs" Rev. Barbara Stephens who gave me the "solutions" to a transformed heart.

Rev. John Kilpatrick who showed me excellence of ministry and shepherded my heart.

Rev. Jonathan Schaeffer who demonstrates the God-kind-of-love every day.

To all the others, too many to name, who have shared my life with the love that keeps on giving.

CONTENTS

INTRODUCTION

Our lives are journey of identity. Know thyself, one famous philosopher said. Why? When we know who we are, we can live in the surety that our lives have purpose and meaning. Knowing who we are gives us a past, a present, and a future. Knowing who we are eliminates a lot of trials and errors that may side slap us and even lead us to ruin and despair.

Knowing who we are gives us more than a sense of our own personal gifts, traits, and abilities. We are more than the sum of our parts. We are a part of a greater whole, giving significance and purpose to a greater picture.

Knowing who we are fulfills the deepest needs of our heart. We know where we belong. We know we are not alone. We know we are accepted and even celebrated. We don't have to hide or seek. We know our lives have meaning, purpose and value.

People throughout time have shared the same struggle: identification, signification, and spiritual connection. In the end, every culture has looked to spiritual leaders to provide answers and even pathways to personal fulfillment. And, for the most part, the answers have been self-defeating. We cease to be human beings, and have become human doings, believing we must earn the place, the love, and the rewards we so earnestly crave.

The gospel of Jesus Christ is the only path that offers a "come as you are" invitation to the spiritual kingdom we are seeking. Our hearts long to connect with our most "significant other"—our maker, Father, and God.

The invitation is different from all others because it is a sure thing—we are accepted in the beloved now, without any reservation, without any stipulations or conditions, without any demands. Jesus Christ became like us, laying down His divinity, so that we could become like Him. And He's doing all the work!

Our part is to cooperate, yield, and agree—from the heart. This is the only cost to us, the only currency acceptable in this Kingdom. Believing with our heart, not simply with our minds, that Jesus Christ redeemed us by His perfect sacrifice at the cross of Calvary gives us access to the deepest yearnings of our hearts—significance, purpose, and intimacy with God.

Believing that Jesus did not stay in the grave, but was resurrected from the dead, assures us that we, too, have been given a new life. Now in Christ we are a new creation, members in good standing of the family of God.

Through revelation from the Holy Spirit, we begin to understand that the resurrection of Jesus Christ is the pivotal truth that transforms our lives. Resurrection is the power of transformation. Resurrection is about death and life, old life and new. Resurrection is the realization of our greatest hopes.

When our hearts accept Jesus' gift of life, a transformation takes place in us. It is a miracle of identification. Now, when we invite Jesus to be Lord of our life, His resurrection becomes a part of our identity as well.

The Bible says that we were raised with Him (Col. 2:12). Redemption is a finished work. Most of us don't understand the full value of redemption. We accept it as simply a "payment of our sins," but redemption is more than that.

Redemption is the door to the Kingdom of God, the kingdom that has always existed. This is the kingdom of goodness and love, acceptance and provision, power and authority where we now may abide in our everyday lives.

When Jesus came to redeem us, He did not just fix what was broken. What redemption brought was a new creation with a new life. On earth we are born into a family, a culture, a race, an economic position, a political system, and, often, a religious tradition. Our earthly state comes with a family, rights, authority, privileges, and obligations. These are the roots of our identity, our purpose, and our significance.

When we are born again in Christ we take on a new state or condition. It is the state of Christness. We have a new family and a new identity with new rights, new authority, new privileges, new language, and new opportunities.

Our "old" nature, born in corruption, is now buried with Christ in His death. His own resurrection life is now vital, now alive in us. We have a new heart and a new life. Actually, we now possess treasures old and new, for we lose nothing good in the exchange.

As a new creation, we may now partake of the very nature of God, the nature of Jesus, now our recognized Brother as well as our Savior and Lord. That nature is supernatural, spiritual, and identical to the nature of Christ Himself. He is our Brother, and we share the same Father. He has brought us home. We are now legally God's sons and daughters and we can have the intimacy our heart craves with our Father.

In Christ, we experience "Christness," the state or condition of Christ. The Bible puts it simply: "Therefore if any man be in Christ, he is a new creature: old things are passed away; behold, all things are become new" (2 Cor 5:17, KJV). The condition of Christ is ours by the great exchange through faith.

The traditions of man and our old way of thinking would call that impossible. Religion tries to reach God by acts of obedience to rules, regulations, and divine laws. Religion, by this definition, cannot free us. We need the power of resurrection.

Twelve is the number of God's government. The life of Christ in me now transforms my own new life. So I have chosen a familiar tune, "The 12 Days of Christmas," to structure this exploration of our new identity by the rebirth. The new song is entitled "The 12 Days of *Christness.*" It is song I sing in joy and expectation. It is a song of faith that we can all sing as we grow from glory to glory one day at a time.

That's what *12 Days, New Creation Transformations* is about. This "sacred secret," as St. Paul calls it, will change your life as you allow it to permeate your paradigms, puncture your previous positions, and pattern new pathways for a prosperous, potent walk of power!

RELATED SCRIPTURES

(Isa. 43:19 AMP) Behold, I am doing a new thing! How it springs forth; do you not perceive and know it and will you not give heed to it? I will even make a way in the wilderness and rivers in the desert.

(2 Cor. 5: 16-17 AMP) Therefore if any person is [engrafted] in Christ (the Messiah) he is a new creation (a new creature altogether); the old [previous moral and spiritual condition] has passed away. Behold, the fresh and the new has come! But all things are from God, Who through Jesus Christ reconciled us to Himself [received us into favor, brought us into harmony with Himself] and gave to us the ministry of reconciliation [that by word and deed we might aim to bring others in harmony with Him].

(Gen. 1:25 AMP) And God said, Let Us [Father, Son, and Holy Spirit] make man in Our image, after Our likeness: and let them have complete authority over the fish of the sea, the birds of the air, the [tame] beasts, and over all the earth, and over everything that creeps upon the earth.

(Gal. 2:20 AMP) I have been crucified with Christ [in Him I have shared His crucifixion]: it is no longer I who live, but Christ (the Messiah) lives in me; and the life I now live in the body I live by faith in (by adherence to and reliance on and complete trust in) the Son of God, Who loved me and gave Himself up for me.

THE TWELVE DAYS OF CHRISTNESS

On the first day of Christness, my Lord, He gave to me
a New Heart ablaze with His love.

On the second day of Christness, my Lord, He gave to me
two Great Lights.

On the third day of Christness, my Lord, He gave to me
three Kingdom Keys.

On the fourth day of Christness, my Lord, He gave to me
four Living Gospels.

On the fifth day of Christness, my Lord, He gave to me
five Signs and Wonders.

On the sixth day of Christness, my Lord, He gave to me
six Pieces of Armor.

On the seventh day of Christness, my Lord, He gave to me
seven Gifts for Giving.

On the eighth day of Christness, my Lord, He gave to me
eight 'Tudes with Promise.

On the ninth day of Christness, my Lord, He gave to me
nine Fruits of the Spirit.

On the tenth day of Christness, my Lord, He gave to me
ten Horns a Blowing.

On the eleventh day of Christness, my Lord, He gave to me
eleven New Birth Blessings.

On the twelfth day of Christness, my Lord, He gave to me
twelve Months to Praise Him.

The secret to transformation

is

Seeing yourself in the book!

On the first day of CHRISTNESS,
my Lord, He gave to me

A NEW HEART ABLAZE WITH HIS LOVE

A new heart also will I give you, and a new spirit will I put within you: and I will take away the stony heart out of your flesh, and I will give you an heart of flesh (Ezekiel 36:26 KJV).

HEART:

(1)   THE **CENTER** OF A PERSON'S EMOTIONS OR INMOST THOUGHTS; KNEW IT IN HER HEART

(2)   THE **ABILITY** TO FEEL EMOTIONS OR AFFECTION; A TENDER HEART,

(3)   **COURAGE**; TAKE HEART,

(4)   **ENTHUSIASM;** HIS HEART ISN'T IN IT,

(5)   **A BELOVED PERSON**; DEAR HEART,

(6)   THE **INNERMOST PART** OF A THING, THE CLOSE COMPACT HEAD, THE HEART OF THE MATTER; **THE VITAL PART** OF IT.[1]
(emphasis, mine)

NOW

*We are a **new creation**.*

Old things are passed away.

Everything is NEW.

We will learn a whole new way

Of being, Of living,

Of relating to ourselves and to one another,

And, of course, to our Father, God--

The way of the Spirit.

*Our **Center** is Christ in us;*

*Our **Ability** is Christ in us,*

*Our **Courage** is Christ in us;*

*Our **Enthusiasm** is Christ in us;*

*He is the **Beloved Person** who abides in us;*

*He is our **Vital Part.***

The heart of the matter is this: Can God really love me and have a relationship with me? Here's a common dialog. It is not unlike my own when I encountered Jesus more than 20 years ago. It goes something like this:

I have risked loving and believing so many times, and it always resulted in heartbreak. I believed mom and dad when they said they loved me, but then they rejected me and disappointed me. I believed my best friend, and that was the person who betrayed my trust and broke my heart. In fact, everyone in whom I have believed has either disappointed and hurt me in some way or downright betrayed me. And I've learned that things change, people change, and you can't trust anyone.

I even believed the church teachers, but when the rubber met the road and my life fell apart, I felt their condemnation and rejection. Why would God let that happen if He really loved me?

How can it be true that He really loves me without any strings attached? There is always some kind of condition. It began with my parents, and then as I grew older it included everyone else who said they loved me—they wanted it their way or I pay.

I just know that God wouldn't take me as I am—I need to clean up my life first, then maybe I'll bring my life to Him. I'll never be good enough.

I'm not ready to change right now. I can't come up to

His standard anyway. I've tried. It's just not my time. I don't feel any different when I pray.

Oh, I know God really exists, but how can it be that He really knows the number of hairs on my head. I lose countless hairs each time I brush or even wash my hair! And what makes you think He even cares?

Besides, there are lots more important things that need His attention than *my* needs or desires. I can handle my life. Let Him take care of the really needy ones.

Do you mean that God not only forgives my every sin, but blots them out from His memory? No one can do that. There's always a payback. I can't take the risk. There's got to be a catch. I grew up in church. There's nothing in it for me. I don't fit into that mold; in fact, I don't fit into any mold. And you know what? I don't want to!

What do you mean, I don't have to? He wants me? Like this? He loves me? Like this? He'll use me? Like I am? I don't have to be like you or her or him? I can just be me? No payback? Jesus paid it? Walk and talk with Him? Lean on Him? He's faithful? Even when I'm not?

Just as I am, Lord Jesus, please come into my heart....

Perhaps you know someone with a similar story. We all have a testimony, whether it be of faith or unbelief. The heart of the matter is that God wants to give us a new heart, a heart that is the very image and nature of His own. He wants to become the very center of our lives.

He also wants to become the ability that works within us to make His promises real to us. There's more to the Kingdom of

God than just the "world to come." There's the Kingdom of God that is *here and now*, that we may enjoy and confidently draw upon. There is a *now* Kingdom of God that we can learn to live in at this present time. It begins as a new life in our heart.

The Bible has a lot to say about the heart. It says that the heart of man is wicked and deceitful, full of selfishness and pride. That is the heart that you and I were born with. Our hearts are imperfect, with beliefs about ourselves and our relationships that may not be true. As we grow, we build walls around our hearts to protect them from the hurts and disappointments that will surely come.

As children, our hearts learn quickly that the moms and dads who conceived us also fall short of the perfect mark of love. Our hearts learn early to self-protect and to hide from intimacy.

The heart of a child is self-centered. Demanding attention and already knowing what we want or don't want, our young hearts are determined to be satisfied. Some never outgrow that level of maturity.

Later, as adolescents we love those who make us feel good about ourselves; we love those who meet our needs and desires. The love that we defined as a child often continues to frame our world in later years. It is centered on our self and our need.

Many adults never reach beyond that kind of love. For those that do learn that love is more than a feeling, more than serving one's own needs, love becomes a commitment and a covenant shared.

But what usually happens in our adult lives is that we

haven't had a true change of heart. Our own heart-needs demand satisfaction and we come into conflict with the heart-needs and desires of others. If these conflicts remain unresolved, we have a change-of-heart. Then our commitments die. Our hearts may experience bitterness, pain, rejection, and, finally, isolation. Our hearts become like stone—hard and impenetrable.

The story of my heart followed this pattern, too. My life before resurrection was a story of failed relationships, betrayal, and disappointment with myself as well as with others. Shame and self-blame kept me separated from receiving love or affirmation. Believing lies about God and about my own heart-identity isolated me and eventually destroyed my hope.

My story didn't have a good prognosis for success and well-being until I gave away what I was holding on to so tightly—my battered, bruised, broken, and boarded-up heart. Giving that up was like dying for me. Even though my life was like was the dregs of a dream gone dry, the death of a vision glazed with decay and infection, it was *me*. It was all I had. But I was desperately sad, and so I gave it away. By then there was nothing to lose. No great gift to God was my life, but He didn't reject it or belittle it.

When I finally succumbed to the love of God at the age of thirty-three, I offered to Him only that which remained—ruins upon ruins, and a heart of stone. But it was all He needed to begin a transformation that would recreate a life, a world, and a future that looked altogether impossible from where I had been standing. (You'll get all the details of that transformation in "Day 4, Four Living Gospels.") I got a new heart for the old one, and a new life to go with it.

Our hearts are ruled by self-desire and personal ambition from birth through death unless we experience a radical transformation. Person-to-person encounters won't produce the kind of radical change of heart I'm talking about here.

Encounters with ideas or mindful things cannot produce a heart–transformation that sustains peace, joy, or faith either. Our culture seems to think that an education is the key to future success. Though exercising the mind can profit some, it is the issues of the heart that really determine the present and the future of a person's life. Our minds believe only what our heart filters to be true. *Everything begins in the heart.*

The Bible says that out of the abundance of the heart the mouth speaks (Matt 12:34). The mind may be the battlefield where one thought vies for authority over another thought, but the mind is only a computer that accumulates, sorts, and categorizes. It is a slave to our hearts. Our *hearts* determine what our mind believes to be *true*.

The thoughts that we entertain the most are the thoughts that shape our self-concepts, our relationships, our hopes and dreams. *And those thoughts are determined by the condition of the heart.* We all need the filter of *Christness* to separate truth from lie, real from circumstance, life from death. Adam and Eve's hearts withered when they believed the lie they heard from one who would destroy their lives. That lie was that God would withhold good from them and that self-reliance was a God-kind-of-life. It is the lie that has also keeps us separated from God.

At their very best our hearts are self-centered and self-

serving. The best we can offer to the world is corru
center. Our hearts by nature are wicked, deceitful, an selfish
(Matt 15:19). The thoughts and motivations that issue from them
cannot fulfill or satisfy the deep longings that tug at our hearts.
We are like a ship that is wind-tossed, bending to and fro with
each new wave, at the mercy of the winds of change. Without
anchor, our hearts yearn for unconditional love, for intimacy
without wounds, for freedom to be ourselves without fear.

The Bible speaks of the "imagination of the heart" (Gen
8:11, Jer 7:24, 2 Cor 10:5), believing the lie rather than the truth.
The Bible uses words like overwhelmed, failing, erring, and
desolate to describe our unrenewed hearts. It says our hearts are
dry, deceived, and rebellious. Our hearts are slow to believe,
envious, broken, grieved, and unbelieving, just as mine was. The
fruit of that old life was a heart that became discouraged,
hardened, defensive, and fearful. So many hearts become
despairing and stony as lives unfold without the touch of Christ's
transforming power.

But now there's really GOOD NEWS! The Transformer
has come! He has offered the great exchange. And it's for
everyone! He has promised to take our stony heart and give us a
"heart of flesh."

One of the first works of the transformation of the New
Birth is a New Heart. This is not a heart like our old one. The
Word of God calls it a "heart of flesh." That means soft. We say
tenderized, caring, compassionate, vulnerable, and at peace.

This new heart is the heart of the Father. It is a
supernatural heart, made in God's holy image and His very

nature. It's a heart that can give and receive the same kind of love that our Father God gives.

The Bible uses words like soft, upright, perfect, and merry to describe this new heart. It calls it wise, willing, believing, humble, and pure. Our new hearts are also confident, understanding, and clean. The Bible says that the recreated heart is established and enlarged. The Bible calls our new heart sound, fat, one, purposed, honest, and good. These are the words that the Bible uses to describe the condition of the New Heart. It's a "suddenly" that takes a lifetime to really understand.

We may not "feel" the transformation emotionally when it occurs, but it is a fact nonetheless. Jesus calls the transformation "born again" (John 3.2-5). When our spirit is regenerated, the nature of God comes to make its home in us. Now that doesn't mean we *become* gods; it means, to use my new word, "*Christness*," the condition of Christ by His indwelling and Lordship of our lives.

Our new heart is the heart of our Father. Let's take a look at His heart and the kind of love that flows from it. If we examine 1 Corinthians 13, the "Love chapter," perhaps we can begin to understand the love of the Father.

> ...if I ...have not love (God's love in me), I gain nothing. Love endures long and is patient and kind; love never is envious nor boils over with jealousy, is not boastful or vainglorious, does not display itself haughtily. It is not conceited (arrogant and inflated with pride): it is not rude' (unmannerly) and does not act unbecomingly. Love (God's love in us) does not insist on its own rights or its own way, for it is not self-seeking; it

is not touchy or fretful or resentful; it takes no account of the evil done to it [it pays not attention to a suffered wrong]. It does not rejoice at injustice and unrighteousness, but rejoices when right and truth prevail. Love bears up under anything and everything that comes, is ever ready to believe the best of every person, its hopes are fadeless under all circumstances, and it endures everything [without weakening]. Love never fails [never fades out or becomes obsolete or comes to an end].

(2 Cor. 13:3b-8a AMP)

Human love can never reach this standard consistently. Though we may attempt to reach this standard, our old self-serving hearts get in the way, and we fall short of the goal of giving love. Our Father's love *for* us and *in* us is BIG! There's room enough for us to grow, to make mistakes, to trust, to ask, to weep, to laugh, and to be real.

That's called "agape" in the Bible. *Strongs's Concordance* defines it this way: "agape love, i.e. affection or benevolence; a love-feast:—(feast of) charity, dear, love" (Strongs, G26). Wow! "A love feast!" Our Father's love is a love feast. Now that's something we can "sink our teeth into." [Sic]

All joking aside, we haven't even begun to realize the height and the depth and the breadth of His love. "However, as it is written: 'No eye has seen, no ear has heard, no mind has conceived what God has prepared for those who love him'—but God has revealed it to us by his Spirit. The Spirit searches all things, even the deep things of God" (1 Cor 2:9-10 NIV).

He will guide us into all things. He will pray for us when

we don't know how to pray ourselves. The Holy Spirit, the third person of the Godhead, will take head knowledge and turn it into Heart knowledge. Out of the heart come the issues of life. Now we can embrace a new kind of love that can give and receive without fear or condition.

Our Father's heart for us is perfect, and His love for us will never change. It is not dependent on circumstances or anything we do or don't do. Our own heart is being transformed into His image, and we are growing into perfection and maturity. We are in a process. That's why we see so many Christians who fall short of the Father's perfect heart. God's not done with them yet!

Now as a new creation we learn to look to God for our vitality, our strength, our needs, our peace, and our joy. Our Father has provided everything for us in Himself through Jesus Christ, and it belongs to us by the power of resurrection.

When we walk in *Christness*, we are operating in His love, His strength, His peace, His wisdom, His own nature. It is the Father's own nature that can now flow through our lives. We are being transformed by His love. It is a Father's love. It is a Son's and Brother's love. It is perfect love. And it is now *our* love.

Our wholeness, deliverance, healing, salvation, protection and are not dependent on our performance. We don't have to earn this wonderful gift. In fact, we can't. It's utterly impossible for us to earn God's love. We *already have all the love He can give us;* we are His children.

As we grow in *Christness*, our hearts also mature and

manifest the Father's kind of love to others. Jesus takes the stony hard heart that we gave Him and makes it His home one chamber at a time, as we offer it to Him. He just doesn't ignore our old hurts or heart-conditions. When He enters a chamber of our heart, He heals it, and even remodels it! It's part of the gift of wholeness He brings to our lives—all our lives.

The pain, the anger, the hurt, the bitterness, the rage, and the mistrust that once kept us self-protecting and isolated now are swept away and, by our invitation, that chamber is fired up and made ready for a new life! God does all the work at our request, never invading, manipulating, or pressuring us to have His way. That's His kind of love.

God heals our brokenness, and transforms us from the inside out. We don't have to change the "outside," trying to make ourselves better in any way. A change of heart creates the outward changes that naturally follow.

Then He shows us how to guard our new hearts. Obeying or following His lead assures us of His continued presence and power to keep us and to mature us in *Christness*. It's a process, and it is also our choice. We are free will agents; our decisions shape our lives. Our hearts speak the condition of our lives.

Jesus spoke against the priests of His day for their hardness of heart. They knew all the rules, but they had no love for the people, no compassion, no mercy. Part of Jesus' earthly ministry was to show that the Church was not something made by man. It is a body of believes with Jesus Christ as her head, established by God Himself in the kind of "love feast" that excludes no one, condemns no one, and controls no one. Like

13

Jesus Christ, the true Church-body loves the unlovely, nurtures the untouchable, and honors all members in the freedom and the integrity of the Father's love following the lead of her head, Jesus.

It's like a puzzle; each individual is one unique, important piece, and all the pieces fit together to form one unified body with Jesus Christ as the head. The Church exists to reveal the heart of the Father for all the peoples of the earth. God's heart is for us.

Today we are the hands that reach out and love others, the words that beckon the hurting to be healed, the dying to live. The Jesus they will meet is the Jesus in you and in me. Your *Christed* life will lead them to have a personal, dynamic, vital relationship with Him themselves. This is the true church, the one that is in the process of transformation, just like us, her members!

God's heart, His love, His favor, His nature *is* complete, and that is what He offers us in Christ. Just as Jesus Christ identified with us, became sin, and then redeemed us from its slavery, now we are invited to find our new identity in Him. We are invited to make the great exchange—our broken, bruised, battered, bitter, weary, distant, hardened hearts for His. He will take our old heart and make it new again—whole, tender, perfect, wise, believing, confident, clean, willing, pure, purposed, and altogether good. We *are* His priceless treasure. It's time we know that—from the heart!

NOW

*We are a **new creation**.*
Old things are passed away.
Everything is NEW.
We will learn a whole new way
Of being, Of living,
Of relating to ourselves and to one another,
And, of course, to our Father, God--

The way of the Spirit.

*Our **Center** is Christ in us;*
*Our **Ability** is Christ is us,*
*Our **Courage** is Christ in us;*
*Our **Enthusiasm** is Christ in us;*
*He is the **Beloved Person** who abides in us;*
*He is our **Vital Part.***

He has taken out our stony heart and given us
A heart of flesh, His heart.
We've made the great exchange.
Now it's His Kingdom, His life,
His heart that frames our world.
It's a love feast, and there's plenty
Of whatever you want or need.
It's for everyone who asks.

RELATED SCRIPTURES (KJV)

Psa 37:4 Delight thyself also in the LORD; and he shall give thee the desires of thine heart.

Psa 22:26 The meek shall eat and be satisfied: they shall praise the LORD that seek him: your heart shall live for ever.

Psa 51:10 Create in me a clean heart, O God; and renew a right spirit within me

Prov 17:22 A merry heart doeth good like a medicine: but a broken spirit drieth the bones.

Prov 19:21 There are many devices in a man's heart; nevertheless the counsel of the LORD, that shall stand.

Jer 31:33 But this *shall be* the covenant that I will make with the house of Israel; After those days, saith the LORD, I will put my law in their inward parts, and write it in their hearts; and will be their God, and they shall be my people.

Mat 5:8   Blessed are the pure in heart: for they shall see God.

Mat 6:21 For where your treasure is, there will your heart be also.

Mat 12:34 O generation of vipers, how can ye, being evil, speak good things? for out of the abundance of the heart the mouth speaketh .

Mark 7:21 For from within, out of the heart of men, proceed evil thoughts, adulteries, fornications, murders,

John 14:1 Let not your heart be troubled: ye believe in God, believe also in me.

John 14:27 Peace I leave with you, my peace I give unto you: not as the world giveth, give I unto you. Let not your heart be troubled, neither let it be afraid.

Rom 5:5 And hope maketh not ashamed; because the love of God is shed abroad in our hearts by the Holy Ghost which is given unto us.

Rom 10:9 That if thou shalt confess with thy mouth the Lord Jesus, and shalt believe in thine heart that God hath raised him from the dead, thou shalt be saved.

Rom 10:10 For with the heart man believeth unto righteousness; and with the mouth confession is made unto salvation

1 Cor 2:9 But as it is written, Eye hath not seen, nor ear heard, neither have entered into the heart of man, the things which God hath prepared for them that love him.

Gal 4:6 And because ye are sons, God hath sent forth the Spirit of his Son into your hearts, crying, Abba, Father.

Eph 5:19 Speaking to yourselves in psalms and hymns and spiritual songs, singing and making melody in your heart to the Lord;

Eph 6:6 Not with eyeservice, as menpleasers; but as the servants of Christ, doing the will of God from the heart;

Phi 4:7 And the peace of God, which passeth all understanding, shall keep your hearts and minds through Christ Jesus.

1 Thes 3:13 To the end he may establish your hearts unblamable in holiness before God, even our Father, at the coming of our Lord Jesus Christ with all his saints.

Heb 3:12 Take heed, brethren, lest there be in any of you an evil heart of unbelief, in departing from the living God.

Heb 4:12 For the word of God is quick, and powerful, and sharper than any two-edged sword, piercing even to the dividing asunder of soul and spirit, and of the joints and marrow, and is a discerner of the thoughts and intents of the heart.

Heb 8:10   For this is the covenant that I will make with the house of Israel after those days, saith the Lord; I will put my laws into their mind, and write them in their hearts: and I will be to them a God, and they shall be to me a people.

Heb 10:22 Let us draw near with a true heart in full assurance of faith, having our hearts sprinkled from an evil conscience, and our bodies washed with pure water.

1 John 3:21 Beloved, if our heart condemn us not, then have we confidence toward God.

1 John 3:20 For if our heart condemn us, God is greater than our heart, and knoweth all things.

On the second day of CHRISTNESS,
my Lord, He gave to me

TWO
GREAT LIGHTS

And God made two great lights; the greater light to rule the day, and the lesser light to rule the night: he made the stars also (Gen 1:16 KJV).

When Jesus spoke again to the people, he said, "I am the light of the world. Whoever follows me will never walk in darkness, but will have the light of life" (John 8:12 NIV).

"You are the light of the world. A city on a hill cannot be hidden. Neither do people light a lamp and put it under a bowl. Instead they put it on its stand, and it gives light to everyone in the house. In the same way, let your light shine before men, that they may see your good deeds and praise your Father in heaven (Mat 5:14-16 NIV).

The Lord God created two great natural lights in the heavens. These great lights represent His presence on the earth: the greater light, the sun, and the lesser light, the moon.

There is an order to things. In the solar system, the earth and other planets with their satellites revolve around the sun, the source of illumination and heat, activating life. As these bodies absorb the sun's rays, they are both physically and chemically transformed. Not only are the things that were previously hidden exposed, but these heavenly bodies themselves are also transformed by the illumination process of the sun.

One has only to consider the life process of a seed to understand the power of the illumination of the sun. Plants provide the ultimate source of food for nearly all organisms on earth. Light is necessary to first warm the seed so that it can germinate. Without adequate heat the vitality of the seed remains only in the potential state. Once germinated, the seed begins to sprout and the seedling produces a stem that reaches upward toward the light, the source of the life- giving substance.

As this seedling grows into a visible plant, the light of the sun activates the energy cycle that creates not only food for the plant, but also water and oxygen for the environment. Because energy is constantly being lost as heat, the cycle requires constant input of light energy for its continued functioning. This process is known as "photosynthesis. Photosynthesis converts light energy into chemical energy. What that means to us is that light is a vital force, a force that not only initiates the life process, but also transforms it into a more complex substance.

In the process of growth, the seed, becoming a mature plant, has as its primary function reproduction. Now the light of the sun is so powerful that a simple organism like a plant (or a man) cannot be exposed to its rays directly. The ultraviolet radiation would decompose it readily when struck by the high-energy photons of ultraviolet light. In fact, without the shielding effects of the atmosphere, life on earth could not develop.

Too much direct light would destroy the seed; too little light would hinder and even prevent plant maturation and eventual reproduction.

God has provided the seed with the substances it needs to thrive, as well as the protection it needs to survive. Light, water, and earth minerals in the right combination produce an organism that will manifest its potential and even reproduce in strength.

Both Luke and Matthew relate the parable of the seed. This parable told by Jesus illustrates the seed principle both in the natural and spiritual kingdoms. Here is the parable from the book of Luke:

> And when a great multitude were coming together, and those from the various cities were journeying to Him, He spoke by way of a parable: "The sower went out to sow his seed; and as he sowed, some fell beside the road; and it was trampled under foot, and the birds of the air ate it up. "And other seed fell on rocky soil, and as soon as it grew up, it withered away, because it had no moisture. "And other seed fell among the thorns;

and the thorns grew up with it, and choked it out. "And other seed fell into the good soil, and grew up, and produced a crop a hundred times as great." As He said these things, He would call out, "He who has ears to hear, let him hear. And His disciples began questioning Him as to what this parable might be. And He said, "To you it has been granted to know the mysteries of the kingdom of God, but to the rest it is in parables, in order that seeing they may not see, and hearing they may not understand." Now the parable is this: the seed is the word of God. "And those beside the road are those who have heard; then the devil comes and takes away the word from their heart, so that they may not believe and be saved."And those on the rocky soil are those who, when they hear, receive the word with joy; and these have no firm root; they believe for a while, and in time of temptation fall away. "And the seed which fell among the thorns, these are the ones who have heard, and as they go on their way they are choked with worries and riches and pleasures of this life, and bring no fruit to maturity. "And the seed in the good soil, these are the ones who have heard the word in an honest and good heart, and hold it fast, and bear fruit with perseverance. (Luke 8:4-15 NASB)

In this parable we see the consequences which befell the seed because of the types of soil in which the seed was sown. Light always provided the catalyst for growth, but that growth was determined by the condition of the soil.

The seed is the Word of God (Lk 8:11). The light is the necessary illumination or *revelation* of that Word in our lives.

Jesus reveals that He is the light of the world. "Then spake Jesus again unto them, saying, I am the light of the world: he that followeth me shall not walk in darkness, but shall have the light of life" (Jn 8:12).

The problem is never with the light; it is with the soil. The soil is the ground of our hearts. That means that we have a responsibility for the maintenance and nurturance of the ground that keeps the seed in the garden of our heart. Learning from the parable of the seed, our part is to keep the soil of our heart soft, pure, moist, fresh, and frequently tended. Then the seed planted there will supply us a great harvest of reward.

The Seed is the Word of God, and the Word of God is nothing less than Jesus Christ Himself. "In the beginning was the Word and the Word was with God and the Word was God" (John 1:1). That means that when Jesus enters our heart and takes Lordship over our lives, His own nature and essence can reproduce itself in us. His light develops and nurtures the seed of His spirit to bring it to maturity in our lives—Christ in us, our hope of glory. As we learn and study Scripture, the living Word of God, and share heart-intimacy with God, we grow and mature in *Christness*.

Jesus is the Light of the world of man. Jesus' light illumes and excites every aspect of our being. His abiding presence shining *in* us transforms us into His image and nature. His light shining *on* us reflects the joy and the peace of His love guiding and protecting our lives. And His light shining *through* us transforms and empowers us, bringing life in the widest application to others in His love and His grace. Just as the celestial bodies revolve and receive their life from the sun, we believers revolve and receive our life—body, soul, and spirit—from Jesus.

Now that Jesus abides in us by the power of the Holy Spirit, we, in *Christness*, are becoming the light of the world today. Just as Jesus brought the good news of the gospel in power and demonstration, so we, too, are to shed our light, the light of Christ in us, to the peoples of the earth in power and demonstration of the God-kind-of-love.

Just as one candle dispels one watt of darkness, we as individuals have the power and the (spiritually delegated) legal right to operate in His Name. Jesus told us to take authority over the works of darkness (Mk 16:17, Jn 14:13-14, Jn 16:23). Just as one candle when united with others magnifies the power and magnitude of light, so, too, when we unite with others in *Christness*, the power of unity and agreement *magnifies* the love, the power, and the glory of God on the earth.

God created the moon to bring light to the earth in the dark of night. The moon is the "lesser light" that revolves around the earth. Having no light of its own, its function is to reflect the light of the sun to the earth at night.

Just as the natural sun represents the supernatural Son of God, Jesus Christ, so, too, the moon represents the "lesser light"—the corporate body of believers we usually call "the Church." The Church is not a religious denomination or a set of doctrinal beliefs. The Church is not a building or a set of rules and duties. The Church Jesus created is the lesser light that gets its power and strength directly from the greater light, Jesus.

The Church is living and vital. God calls it the Bride of Christ with Jesus as the groom and husband. (Is 54:5). He also calls it a body with Jesus as the head (Eph 5:23). Each person has a unique function to make the body whole and thriving. There is not one part more important than another. Though there are different functions for different parts of the body, the body of Christ, the Church, was created to operate in complete unity and harmony.

The Church operates as Christ's authorized ambassador on earth. Its mission is to illuminate Jesus' saving work to the world, setting people free and empowering them to walk in intimacy with God. It operates in supernatural, agape love that releases others from all forms of bondage and lack. Jesus' mission statement of Luke 4:18-19 has become our mission statement, too.

Though we are complete in Christ individually, we were created to be corporate, a body of believers where the fullness of the glory of God can be revealed and illuminated. Together, we make up the body of Christ on earth.

The sun's light is always constant, but the moon's illumination goes through phases. History has witnessed the power and love of Christ in waves of revival that touched nations. However, when traditions and legalism (our attempts to earn God's approval through works) replace heartfelt intimacy and reliance upon God, the both the Church and the world suffer.

Staying *Christed* means keeping our heart-connection vital and utterly dependent upon God. The Holy Spirit, who abides in the heart of the believer, is the illuminator of the Word of God. He is the power of resurrection, the same power that raised Jesus from the dead, Who now abides in us. The Holy Spirit activates the Word of God in our hearts, making it our reality. He backs up the Word of God in our lives with power and demonstration when we then speak and act on it in faith.

We are the Church empowered by the Holy Spirit to continue the works of Christ on the earth in the God-kind-of-love. As the Holy Spirit confirms the faith-filled Word with signs and wonders, the Church shall fulfill the Great Commission, heralding the Kingdom of God on earth as it is in heaven, in anticipation of the return of the King of Kings, Jesus Christ.

I like to say that the moon shining in its fullness has a "face." And to my eye, that "face" seems to appear full of joy. Surely, knowing Christ in us, on us, and through us fills us with joy! He is the Light of the world (John 9:8), and He said that now we are also the light of the world (Mt 5:4). He is also illuminating His presence *within* us by virtue of the new birth, the re-creation of our beings in *Christness*. Just as the sun and the moon provide needed light to the earth, Jesus and His body, the Church, shine the nature of God's love and light to the peoples of the earth.

RELATED SCRIPTURES (KJV)

Psa 27:1 A Psalm of David. The LORD is my light and my salvation; whom shall I fear? the LORD is the strength of my life; of whom shall I be afraid?

Psa 119:105 Thy word is a lamp unto my feet, and a light unto my path.

Isa 5:20 Woe unto them that call evil good, and good evil; that put darkness for light, and light for darkness; that put bitter for sweet, and sweet for bitter!

John 1:4 In him was life; and the life was the light of men.

John 8:12 Then spake Jesus again unto them, saying, I am the light of the world: he that followeth me shall not walk in darkness, but shall have the light of life.

Rom 13:12 The night is far spent, the day is at hand: let us therefore cast off the works of darkness, and let us put on the armour of light.

2 Cor 4:4 In whom the god of this world hath blinded the minds of them which believe not, lest the light of the glorious gospel of Christ, who is the image of God, should shine unto them.

Eph 5:8 For ye were sometimes darkness, but now are ye light in the Lord: walk as children of light:

1 Pet 2:9 But ye are a chosen generation, a royal priesthood, an holy nation, a peculiar people; that ye should show forth the praises of him who hath called you out of darkness into his marvellous light:

1 John 1:7 But if we walk in the light, as he is in the light, we have fellowship one with another, and the blood of Jesus Christ his Son cleanseth us from all sin.

1 John 2:10 He that loveth his brother abideth in the light, and there is none occasion of stumbling in him.

Rev 21:23 And the city had no need of the sun, neither of the moon, to shine in it: for the glory of God did lighten it, and the Lamb is the light thereof.

Rom 12:5 So we, being many, are one body in Christ, and every one members one of another.

1 Cor 10:17 For we being many are one bread, and one body: for we are all partakers of that one bread.

1 Cor 12:13-14 For by one Spirit are we all baptized into one body, whether we be Jews or Gentiles, whether we be bond or free; and have been all made to drink into one Spirit. For the body is not one member, but many.

John 17:21-23a That they all may be one; as thou, Father, art in me, and I in thee, that they also may be one in us: that the world may believe that thou hast sent me. And the glory which thou gavest me I have given them; that they may be one, even as we are one: I in them, and thou in me, that they may be made perfect in one;

1 Cor 12:26 –27 And whether one member suffer, all the members suffer with it; or one member be honoured, all the members rejoice with it. Now ye are the body of Christ, members in particular.

"You are the light of the world.

A town built on a hill cannot be hidden.

Neither do people light a lamp and put it under a bowl.

Instead they put it on its stand, and it gives light to everyone in the house.

In the same way, let your light shine before others,

that they may see your good deeds

and glorify your Father in heaven.

Matthew 5:14-16 (NIV)

ISTNESS,
o me

KEYS

ad; and, behold, I am alive
keys of hell and of death (Rev

Then he called his twelve disciples together, and gave **them power and authority over all devils, and to cure diseases** (Luke 9:1 KJV).

Behold, I give unto you power to tread on serpents and scorpions, and **over** *all the power of the enemy: and nothing shall by any means hurt you* (Luke 10:19 KJV).

Who hath delivered us from the power of darkness, and hath *translated us into the kingdom of his dear Son* (Col 1:13 KJV).

And I will give unto thee ***the keys of the kingdom of heaven:*** and whatsoever thou shalt bind on earth shall be bound in heaven: and whatsoever thou shalt loose on earth shall be loosed in heaven (Mat 16:19 KJV).

For verily I say unto you, That whosoever shall say unto this mountain, Be thou removed, and be thou cast into the sea; and shall not doubt in his heart, but shall believe that those things which he saith shall come to pass; *he shall have whatsoever he saith* (Mark 11:23 KJV).

But as many as received him, to them gave he *power to become the sons of God,* even to them that believe on his name (John 1:12 KJV).

For the kingdom of God is not in word, but in *power* (1 Cor. 4:20 KJV).

(italics, mine)

Three is the number that symbolizes God. God is a Trinity: three distinct persons in One God. There are three heavens: on the earth, above the earth, and the abode of the Father. There are three parts to the tabernacle God told Moses to build: the Outer Court, the Inner Court, and the Holy of Holies. Jesus was 30 years old when He began His public ministry and 33 when He died on the cross for our sin. Jesus rose on the Third day. Three is the number that brings Godly things to mind.

Just as natural keys give us access to closed and protected places, God has provided supernatural keys that give us access, protection, and even power to live the life of promise, provision, and peace that is in Him. God gives His keys to His children when they become members of His Kingdom. Jesus said that He is the Door (Jn 10:9). He told us that no man comes to the Father but by Him (Jn 14:6). When we come the Jesus Way, we are given the keys to the Kingdom of God.

The Kingdom is more than a place; it is the very heart of the Father. The first key we receive from God is the key to His heart. This is so remarkable it makes me want to pause with a "Selah." (Like a sigh, "selah" is the word often found at the end of a Davidic psalm which invites us to pause and consider.) Can you imagine the Creator of the universe, the great Jehova-God, the God of our fathers, the God Who spoke through the prophets is the same God Almighty Who wants to invite us to have heart-to-heart intimacy with Him?

When I think that I have received the key to His heart, I am dumbstruck. I cannot imagine that kind of love existed before I knew Him. It took a few years to really believe that He truly loved me without any strings attached. It took trials and tests to prove that He would never reject me when I failed to meet the mark of His desire. But He has convinced me that this is literally true. In the years that I have learned to walk with Him, the power and breadth of His love has transformed my life, and continues to do so. The first key is my dearest treasure. There's nothing on earth to compare to it. And now that kind of love lives in me. The *Christed* life is the life of a new kind of love.

The Bible talks about three kinds of love: fileo, eros, and agape. Fileo is personal affection or liking we have, like brotherly love. Based on feelings, it is subject to change as we change. It is the love that the world knows; it is self-centered and self-fulfilling. The second kind of love in the Bible is called eros. Eros is associated with romantic, sexual love. Like fileo it is not permanent or consistent because it is based on fulfilling a need in ourselves.

With the incarnation of Jesus Christ, a new kind of love came to the earth: agape. (ah-gah'-pay) There is no mention of this word in the Old Testament. It didn't exist on earth until Jesus, the begotten Son of God, brought it to us. It's the very essence of God's heart. It is deliberate, unceasing, unconditional, moral, and holy. It's the love that gives without asking or requiring in return. It's the love that is full of faith and never despairs. It's the love that never ceases, never holds back, and never fails. It's the love that never changes.

The Holy Spirit teaches us about agape in 1 Corinthians. Here's how He describes agape:

> Love is kind and patient, never jealous, boastful, proud, or rude. Love isn't selfish or quick tempered. It doesn't keep a record of wrongs that others do. Love rejoices in the truth, but not in evil. Love is always supportive, loyal, hopeful, and trusting. Love never fails! (1 Cor 13:4-8 CEV)

In other versions of the Bible, the word agape is translated as "charity" to set it apart as the unselfish, giving kind of love.

Agape is the love that covers a multitude of sins (1 Pet 4:8). It is fulfillment of all the Old Testament law, the bond of perfection (Col 3:14). It is the only commandment that Jesus Christ gave us to follow (Jn 13:34). And knowing that we could not do it by our own ability, He gave us His heart together with that God-kind-of-love to fulfill that commandment.

Knowing that trust is earned and progressive, God only dwells in those areas of our hearts and lives that we offer to Him. His kind of love, agape, never takes, but only gives without pause for examination of our worthiness. As As a new creation in Christ through faith, God declares we are righteous and blameless in His sight (Phil 3,9, Rom 3:22, 1Cor 1:8). Agape becomes our standard of love as we grow in *Christness*.

As we become more and more intimate with our Father in Christ, we learn to discern God's voice. Not only do we share our hearts with Him, He shares His with us. God wants us to know His heart and hear His voice. We learn what matters to

Him, and our hearts respond in agape to Him. We find ourselves wanting to say and do what we hear Him saying and doing. This is the way Jesus lived and ministered in His life on earth. It is the way that we come into the *Christed* life, too. In this relationship, we have received another powerful key—the key of agreement.

This is not the agreement of mental assent; it is agreement of the heart founded in agape. It means to give oneself wholly to, holding nothing back. It is the agreement of commitment that will see the thing through. It comes from the Greek word that we get our word "symphony" from. This kind of agreement creates harmony and unity. It is a force that binds together. It is the power of dominion.

Agape agreement creates community, the unity of vision and purpose that supports, builds up, and serves not only the members of that community, but others, too. Amos says, "How can two walk together unless they agree?" (Amos 3:3). Weavers understand the power of agreement. They know that the "warp" and the "woof," the horizontal and vertical threads that make up a fabric, need to be worked together one thread at a time to create a textile that is strong, durable, and beautiful. Agreement is the power of that kind of unity.

The Tower of Babel was constructed out of the power of agreement. God, seeing there would be nothing impossible for them, struck the people with different languages (Gen 11:6-9). This demonstration of the power of agreement outside of the God-kind-of-love warns us of the evils of self-serving love. History has witnessed this power, too. The Crusades, the Holocaust, the genocide of African tribes are just a few examples of the power of agreement apart from God.

But just as evil abounds, so much more does grace abound (Rom 5:20). The power of agreement in the God-kind-of-love is exponentially greater and more powerful than anything man can produce, for it carries within it the very essence of God—agape. Jesus explains it in the Gospels. He is addressing all his disciples, including you and me, because we are His disciples, too, and God is no respecter of persons. What Jesus imparted then, He continues to impart now. He tells them, "And whatever you may ask in My name, that I will do, so that the Father may be glorified in the Son. If you ask anything in My name, I will do it" (John 14:13-14). In another part of the Gospel, Jesus says,

> "Verily I say unto you, what things soever
> ye shall bind on earth shall be bound in heaven;
> and what things soever ye shall loose on earth
> shall be loosed in heaven. Again I say unto you,
> that if two of you shall agree on earth as touching
> anything that they shall ask, it shall be done for
> them of my Father who is in heaven. For where
> two or three are gathered together in my name,
> there am I in the midst of them" (Mat 18:18-20)

This isn't a mandate to speak our wills or even our personal desires. It's not even a "name it and claim it" kind of agreement. Agape agreement that Jesus is referring to *begins* in the Kingdom of God in the Word of the Father. More than even finding a promise in the Word and then giving mental assent to it, agape agreement is walking like Jesus walked, *hearing His Father's voice as He went in heartful agreement and total submission.* Just like Jesus, we can act upon that Word spoken in our hearts and with full confidence, believing that the Lord has done it. As we speak what we have heard from the Lord, we are acting with God to bring His authority over the earth. This brings us to the third Kingdom key—authority.

Jesus Christ came to destroy the works of the devil and to restore to man the dominion he forsook in Eden, the authority over all the earth. Jesus took authority over nature (calming the storm, walking on water), over sickness ("healing them all" (Mat 4:23-4), and over death (raising Lazarus and a young girl from death.) He took authority over demons casting them out from the demoniac and sending them into swine (Mat 8:32). He took authority over over sin and transgression saying, "Your sins are forgiven" (1 John 2:12), "Go and sin no more" (John 8:11).

As heirs and sons of God, as disciples of Jesus Christ, as new creation beings, Jesus gave us a commission with the authority to fulfill it.

> And Jesus came and said to them [the disciples], ·"All authority in heaven and on earth has been given to me. Therefore go and make disciples of all nations, baptizing them in the name of the Father and of the Son and of the Holy Spirit, and teaching them to obey everything I have commanded you. And surely I am with you always, to the very end of the age." (Matt. 28: 18-20 NIV)

Jesus made us His legal representative on this earth. We are not only given authority to teach and to preach the Good News, we are given the same authority that Jesus himself walked with during His ministry on earth. Jesus told His disciples (that's us, too, God being no respecter of persons), "I will give you the keys of the kingdom of heaven, and whatever you bind on earth shall be bound in heaven, and whatever you loose on earth shall be loosed in heaven" (Matt 16:19).

The Lord was not satisfied to give us victory over eternal things only; He also gave us authority over the temporal things as well. The keys that Adam relinquished by unbelief and disobedience are now reclaimed in Jesus Christ's victory for us. As *Christed* ones, may exercise His authority, using His Name to promote His Kingdom on earth.

The authority of the name of Jesus is two-fold. First, it is delegated authority; that is, it is like a power of attorney. The Greek word for this is "exousia." It means "privilege, capacity to enforce when challenged, competence, delegated influence, jurisdiction" (*Strong's Concordance* G1832). It is the office of power, similar, for example to the badge of authority the policeman has to show that he has been delegated authority to maintain the law.

We have been given jurisdiction over all things that pertain to life on earth and in the heavens. In Christ, we have the commission to act in His stead over all of creation for the purpose of fulfilling the work of Christ on earth.

Authority without power is rather useless. A child may be an heir to a great house, but that person won't be given any power until s/he matures and learns how to use it wisely. The same is true for Christians. Authority must be accompanied by power if it is to be effective.

Jesus provided us with that power in the person of the Holy Spirit. He told his disciples to wait in the upper room until they had received power. In Acts 1:8, Jesus says, "But ye shall receive power after that the Holy Ghost has come upon you; and ye shall be witnesses unto me both in Jerusalem, and in all Judea, and in Samaria, and unto the uttermost part of the earth."

The Greek word here for power is "dunamis," literally potentate rule (*Strong's Concordance* G1413). It's God's miracle working power. It's like the gun behind the badge the policeperson wears. Dunamis belongs to the all Kingdom members.

Dunamis can be built up in our spirits after we are born again, and it can be nurtured throughout our lives. That dunamis is the anointing, Christ in us, the abiding presence of the Holy Spirit in our lives. It is built through relationship with God, and developed by exercise.

Dunamis is the power that exercises authority over supernatural powers that torment and arrest us with fear, sickness, poverty, and every form of lack. We have the keys to death and to hell. That means that we can close those doors and stop those forces from tormenting, injuring, stealing, or devastating ourselves and others. Dunamis rose Jesus from the grave; it's the power that Jesus used to heal the sick, cast out demons, and raise the dead. It's the same power that resides now in us. We exercise it through faith and submission to Father God.

Out of our hearts come the issues of life (Pv 4:23); we have what we speak (Mk 11:23). In Christ, as His body, we are carriers that bring hope, peace, faith, joy, healing, and freedom in our words and deeds. We can bring heaven to earth by living and moving in agreement with God's Word. We can speak with the authority of Christ's personal ambassador and activate the promises of God in our own lives and for others, too. In the Name of the Lord, Jesus Christ, whose nature we now share, we are equipped to fulfill the commission of Christ to the world. We are carriers of the God-kind-of-love, spreading the Good News everywhere we go, loving and living a Kingdom kind of life. At least that is the potential we have as *Christed* ones.

God says in Jeremiah, "I know the plans I have for you, plans to prosper you, plans not to harm you, plans to give you a sure hope and a future" (Jer 29:11), Our Father loved us before we loved Him, planned for our abundant life, and provided everything we would ever need or even want. When He sent His Son, Jesus, to save us and to reconcile us back to Himself, He gave Him the keys that we needed.

First, He gave His heart, the agape God-kind-of-love that gives without taking, loves without condition, and keeps without controlling. Second, the key of agreement was birthed out of our shared intimacy. Knowing the Father's heart and desiring His best in all things, we have a part in bringing God's kingdom to earth. The third key, authority, insures us of that victory. Like any muscle, it is developed by virtue of use. The Bible tells us that faith without works is dead (James 2:20). Another translation of this verse is "Show me your faith, I'll show you my works." Faith exercises in authority with expectation.

God honors His Word spoken and exercised in faith. Our part is to follow the direction of the Holy Spirit, and speak the

Word in faith. Knowing that it is God who is doing the work through us, we can begin to reach out beyond mental assent, into the realm of God where all our miracles await us. We are the spout where the glory of God comes out!

We have the keys to the Kingdom of God—agape, agreement, and authority. Jesus Christ gave them to us. He calls it abundant living! We call it Kingdom life! The Holy Spirit in us is the power that backs up the God-Word spoken in faith. The shed blood of Jesus is the atonement of our sin. The Name of Jesus is the power of attorney to promote and enforce the Kingdom of God on this earth. It is our right and our privilege. And it is our high call in Christ.

RELATED SCRIPTURES (KJV)

Col 3:14 And above all these things *put on* charity, which is the bond of perfectness.

1Pe 4:8 And above all things have fervent charity among yourselves: for charity shall cover the multitude of sins.

Jn 3:35 The Father loveth the Son, and hath given all things into his hand.

Rom 13:8 Owe no man any thing, but to love one another: for he that loveth another hath fulfilled the law.

1Joh 4:8 He that loveth not knoweth not God; for God is love.

Mat 5:44 But I say unto you, Love your enemies, bless them that curse you, do good to them that hate you, and pray for them which despitefully use you, and persecute you;

Mat 22:37-39 Jesus said unto him, Thou shalt love the Lord thy God with all thy heart, and with all thy soul, and with all thy mind. This is the first and great commandment. And the second *is* like unto it, Thou shalt love thy neighbor as thyself.

Jn 13:35 By this shall all *men* know that ye are my disciples, if ye have love one to another.

Jn 15:9 As the Father hath loved me, so have I loved you: continue ye in my love.

Jn17:26 And I have declared unto them thy name, and will declare *it*: that the love wherewith thou hast loved me may be in them, and I in them.

Rom 13:10 Love worketh no ill to his neighbor: therefore love *is* the fulfilling of the law.

Gal 5:22-23 But the fruit of the Spirit is love, joy, peace, longsuffering, gentleness, goodness, faith, meekness, temperance: against such there is no law.

2Ti 1:7 For God hath not given us the spirit of fear; but of power, and of love, and of a sound mind.

1Jn 4:8 He that loveth not knoweth not God; for God is love.

Luke 10:19-20 Behold, I give unto you power to tread on serpents and scorpions, and over all the power of the enemy: and nothing shall by any means hurt you. Notwithstanding in this rejoice not, that the spirits are subject unto you; but rather rejoice, because your names are written in heaven.

Jn 1:12 But as many as received him, to them gave he power to become the sons of God, even to them that believe on his name.

Mat 18:19 Again I say unto you, That if two of you shall agree on earth as touching any thing that they shall ask, it shall be done for them of my Father which is in heaven.

2 Co 6:16 And what agreement hath the temple of God with idols? for ye are the temple of the living God; as God hath said, I will dwell in them, and walk in *them*; and I will be their God, and they shall be my people.

Mat 16:19 And I will give unto thee the keys of the kingdom of heaven: and whatsoever thou shalt bind on earth shall be bound in heaven: and whatsoever thou shalt loose on earth shall be loosed in heaven.

Rev 1:18 I am he that liveth, and was dead; and, behold, I am alive forevermore, Amen; and have the keys of hell and of death.

Luke 17:21 Neither shall they say, Lo here! or, lo there! for, behold, the kingdom of God is within you.

Eph 6:12 For we wrestle not against flesh and blood, but against principalities, against powers, against the rulers of the darkness of this world, against spiritual wickedness in high places.

Mat 6:13 And lead us not into temptation, but deliver us from evil: For thine is the kingdom, and the power, and the glory, forever. Amen.

Mat 10:1 And when he had called unto *him* his twelve disciples, he gave them power *against* unclean spirits, to cast them out, and to heal all manner of sickness and all manner of disease.

Mat 28:18 And Jesus came and spake unto them, saying, All power is given unto me in heaven and in earth.

Luk 10:19 Behold, I give unto you power to tread on serpents and scorpions, and over all the power of the enemy: and nothing shall by any means hurt you.

Jn1:12 But as many as received him, to them gave he power to become the sons of God, *even* to them that believe on his name:

Jn10:18 No man taketh it from me, but I lay it down of myself. I have power to lay it down, and I have power to take it again. This commandment have I received of my Father.

Act 1:8 But ye shall receive power, after that the Holy Ghost is come upon you: and ye shall be witnesses unto me both in Jerusalem, and in all Judea, and in Samaria, and unto the uttermost part of the earth.

ENCOURAGE ME!

"Power! That is the essence of the gospel. A powerless gospel preacher is like an unwashed soap salesman. Singing "There is power, power, wonder-working power in the precious blood of the Lamb" and then having to fast and pray for a month to get power does not add up." [2]

Reinhard Bonnke
from *Mighty Manifestations*

"We need to realize that the devil is defeated. He is not omnipresent and he is a creation, not creator. These simple truths will help us to see clearly that prayer must be used primarily to fellowship with the Lord and to spend time being filled up in His presence. Then out of an overflow of His touch, we minister to the needs of hurting humanity." [3]

Dr. Rodney Howard-Browne
from *The Touch of God*

"God has not limited us, but we have limited ourselves by not fully believing in what He is willing to do through us. He is causing some greater things to be birthed in us, faith to believe for the harvest, faith to declare His purposes in all the Earth, faith to speak out for revival." [4]

Ruth Ward Heflin
from *Revival Glory*

On the fourth day of Christness,
My Lord, He gave to me

FOUR LIVING GOSPELS
MATTHEW, MARK, LUKE, & JOHN

And this gospel of the kingdom shall be preached in all the world for *a witness unto all nations;* and then shall the end come (Mat 24:14 KJV).

And he said unto them, Go ye into all the world, and preach the gospel *to every creature.* (Mark 16:15 KJV)

The Spirit of the Lord is upon me, because he hath anointed me to preach the gospel to the poor; he hath sent me to heal the brokenhearted, to preach deliverance to the captives, and recovering of sight to the blind, *to set at liberty them that are bruised* (Luke 4:18 KJV).

But as many as received him, to them gave he power *to become the sons of God,* even to them that believe on his name (John 1:12 KJV).

Jesus answered, Verily, verily, I say unto thee, Except a man be born of water and of the Spirit, he cannot *enter into the kingdom of God* (John 3:5 KJV).

But these are written, that ye might believe that Jesus is the Christ, the Son of God; and that believing *ye might have life through his name* (John 20:31 KJV). [italics mine]

The Gospels—

Eyewitness accounts

> *of the life,*
> *the ministry*
> *and the words*
> *of Jesus Christ,*

Imparting

> *Faith*
> *in the risen Messiah*
> *and Vision*
> *in the life of a believer.*

"Gospel" *means* ***"good news."***

How does good news make you feel?

Why, happy, of course!

Once you get it, you want to ***pass it on!***

The words, evangelism, evangelical, and evangelize are modern day derivatives of the word, "euaggelizo," which means to announce good news, to declare, bring, show glad tidings, to preach the gospel. Though most of us can name a famous evangelist, have heard of evangelical churches, and generally support evangelism in foreign countries, we ourselves are not directly generally impacted by "euaggelizo."

Perhaps we think we know what the "good news" is. Perhaps we have concluded that the gospel has little or no relevance for our daily lives. Some may think that the "good news" is really "bad news" bringing condemnation or a deadbeat life of boredom and predictability. That wasn't the gospel.

Some women, like me, did not want to become "church ladies" because they seemed more like paper cutout dolls, two dimensional figures, and not real people with real issues in their lives. We could not identify with that kind of "good news." That wasn't the gospel.

Some men could not relate to Jesus as a man, a mentor, or Lord. He may have seemed too "out of this world," unrealistically one-dimensional, historical, or simply unapproachable. That wasn't the gospel.

There are four gospels in the Bible that have been recognized for centuries. These are not the only gospels that were written, for others had been witnesses of Jesus Christ, but these four are believed to be the living Word of God written under the inspiration and direction of the Holy Spirit Himself.

Examining the basics of the Bible may give us some insight and appreciation of the Father's love that provides for us what we could not regain by our own efforts and good works. First, we'll take a look at where it all started, even before creation of the universe! It's an incredible picture of God's love for us. It's the gospel, the good news!

Some think that before Jesus was the Son of God, He was the Word of God. (John 1) He was not a separate person but, together with the Holy Spirit, existed as one God in the Father. The *kenosis*, the emptying out or separation into three distinct persons, only occurred as a result of the expression of God's love becoming manifest on our behalf. Why would God do this? Isn't wholeness our personal goal? Weren't we created in God's own image?

Jesus, the Word, was begotten of God and became a person called the Son of God; the life-force or breath of God became a person we call the Holy Spirit. Both proceeded from the Father. The Trinity is the outcome of the love and provision of God manifesting for our sakes. Jesus is the Redeemer who would reconcile fallen children to the Father. The Holy Spirit is the breath of God who would guide, empower, and comfort us in our journey. Our Father God made every provision for our life with Him, a life of wholeness and intimacy, even in spite of the fall that would separate us from Him. The Trinity is also a picture of family living as one in unconditional love. That is the Father's heart for us all.

At the "fullness of time," Jesus was the Seed that the

Spirit of God planted into Mary's virgin womb. Not only is that the literal truth, it also provides a picture of how God Himself brings Christ into our own lives. Jesus is the Seed that the Holy Spirit plants into our spirit when we are born again. The Breath of God is the power of God to create life. It was the Holy Spirit who breathed upon the earth bringing life force into the creation.

It was the Sprit of God who caused us to cry out for our Redeemer, Jesus. We did not initially seek Him, He sought us (1 John 4:19; 1 Cor. 12:3). The Holy Spirit brought us back to the source of our life, our strength, our wisdom, our peace, our joy and our purpose—Jesus. And Jesus made the way for us to come home to our Father.

He knew that sin's nature had warped our minds so we would be self-dependent, not God-dependent. He knew that our emotions and our hearts lied to us. We were wrapped up in shame and blame. We believed lies that God didn't care about us. He knew that our hearts were too hard to lay down our broken lives. He knew that trust and faith issues kept us separated from the Father. He knew we would not seek a God we neither knew nor trusted.

God did not create us that way in the beginning. We were made in His image and likeness with eyes and ears to see and hear His Word and His vision. He created us with the same kind of mind and emotions He has so we could share in the family life and business. We were created for a rich inheritance and a future of prosperity in every dimension of life—spirit, soul, and body.

God created us to be like Him (Gen 1:27). Adam and Eve had bodies like their Father's—full of God's glory, His presence and His power. They walked and talked with God in the garden of delight. That means that they also had the light of revelation. They had knowledge and understanding of the things of God. Adam named all the creatures of the earth. To name something is to know its essence. God gave them the keys to the kingdom they were living in. They were God's caretakers, not servants, but His son and daughter. They had ownership in the family business. They were beings of the God-class.

They walked in the revelation of God's love and goodness. They knew His power and enjoyed His provision. They weren't mindless creatures of instinct. Adam and Eve knew God and shared intimacy with Him, especially Adam who walked with Him every evening.

God gave Adam and Eve one limit: He told Adam not to eat of the tree of knowledge of good and evil (Gen 2:17). Adam and Eve had no consciousness of sin until they disobeyed God's one restriction. Eve was tricked by the serpent, but Adam was not. Eve believed the false revelation of the serpent, believing the deceits that Satan had planted in her heart. Adam knew that to disobey God was no less than treason, no less than becoming an ally to the deceiver against God.

The consequences were dire. They were driven out of the garden. Sin consciousness caused their minds and hearts to draw away from God (Gen 3:10). The glory they shared with their Father they now had left behind as they learned to live by the sweat of their brow with suffering and pain. Now they became slaves to the deceiver. They had given him the deed to the earth by allying with him against God. Now a veil separated them from that place of intimacy, safety, and rest— their Father's kingdom. That veil was rent at the cross (Mat 27:51).

Our own eternal spirit was also separated from God. Losing its glory, our bodies became mortal and our hearts became coated in fear, guilt, and shame. Like Adam and Eve, we don't believe that God will take care of us, and we don't trust Him. The foundation of our lives is built on lies that are then coated with shame. We can't approach God because of that fear and shame and lack of trust. We have become slaves to carnal minds which are darkened by corruption (Rom 8:7).

The dilemma hasn't changed through the ages. As a consequence of Adam and Eve's rebellion, we are born on earth separated from God. We struggle to have a life of faith. We try to earn a life that will make us feel worthy to approach God. Our lack of trust prevents us from discerning His unconditional love as Truth. We need a touch of God in the person of Jesus Christ.

Jesus is the Revelation and the Incarnation of God's love and His will for our lives. His life as a man revealed the Father's true love and heartfelt intent to have intimacy with us. At the cross, Jesus ransomed us by offering a perfect sacrifice for all the sin that had or would ever be committed (Eph 1:7-8). That way, Satan the deceiver, could not have the legal hold of God's children that he had gained at the fall of Adam.

Jesus is the Incarnation, the supernatural birth of the God-man who would bring us back home to our Father and to life in His kingdom. Jesus is all God; He is the living Word, the true God, the Son of the Father. He is also all man; he shared the same nature and being that we possess (Heb 4.15). He became like us, but without sin. He was tempted, but he overcame by the power of the Spirit who resided in Him. He did not live as God on earth, but as a man who was filled with the immeasurable supply of the Holy Spirit. He did that to show us how to live as a "new man," a person of the God-class, one born again by God's Spirit (Mat 10:8).

The good news is that when we simply embrace Christ as our personal savior and Lord, the revelation, or unveiling, of the Father's mind and heart toward us brings us into renewed relationship (Eph 2:8). We are literally recreated in the God-image, the God-nature that was the Father's intent. We regain eternal life in His presence through Christ (Eph 2:6). As we grow in this new state of grace, the revelation of His love and life in us increases our capacity to receive and to give that love. Each new revelation of Christ in us shows us how to live and move in His power and goodness. We literally become "new creatures" (2 Cor 5:17).

Who was the first to hear the good news? Adam and Eve! The fig leaves they had sewn together to cover themselves to hide their sin provided no good thing—no comfort, no durability, and lots and lots of discomfort. The Father provided a covering for them by a blood sacrifice. He made them both long tunics of animal skins. This served both as an immediate provision and as a sign of the coming Redeemer who would cover their sins and even wash them away forever with His own blood (Gen 3:21). When God covered them with the skins of an animal, He showed them His mercy by providing for them what they could not give to themselves. And He provided a promise of a blood sacrifice that would cover their sin and restore them to the kingdom.

By this act, God "cut" a covenant, an eternal promise of protection and provision, between Himself and Adam and all Adam's descendents to provide a redeemer. Justice demanded a consequence for disobedience, but God showed mercy, too. Many question why a good God would demand such a heavy consequence for disobedience. We think of the Father as terrible and fearful, a God of vengeance and violence. We don't understand the underlying character of God that never changes, and is always proactive in our favor. The "law of the seed" may offer new understanding.

The transgression of Adam and Eve set into motion the law of the seed which is one of the impersonal laws by which God created the universe. The law of the seed is also known as the law of sowing and reaping (2 Cor 9.6); scientists call it the law of balance or attraction: for every action there must be a similar reaction. Others call it the law of cause and effect.

When Adam and Eve sinned against God and ate from the tree of the knowledge of good and evil, the consequences were devastating. They exchanged the tree of the life of God-dependence for the tree of the life of legalism and earned rewards. Like a deadly disease, the seed of that fruit, that action, caused them to become mortal and self-reliant. Subject to deception, they created their own belief systems based on lies and half-truths by which they tried to appease an "angry" God. Legally, now, Adam and Eve and all their seed (you and I) were under the rulership and control of the deceiver, the declared enemy of God Almighty (Jn 10:10). Disease, death, deception, distress, and dread became the hallmarks of our new life.

We were kidnapped by a foe who knew the laws of God. We were deceived by a foe who wanted possession of the world God had created for His sons and daughters. We were captured by a foe who made us slaves to a corrupt nature whose only future was distress, disease, and death.

God could only redeem us, or ransom us, legally. The payment had to meet the demands of Justice, because that is God's nature. The enemy did not have to give us up until that price was paid. He knew that the ransom had to come through one of the sons of Adam. Satan (one of his many names) thought he had really hurt God by stealing His children. But God's love is so great, so big, so giving, that He paid the ransom with His own perfect life, in the person of His Son, Jesus Christ (Jn 3:16).

Satan had no legal leg to stand on. The ransom was a man's blood with nothing of the deceiver, of sin, in Him, Jesus, God's true Son, the second Adam (1 Cor 15:45). Satan lost the prize possession which he had stolen from God—the sons and daughters of God. Our Father, God, restored His gift of eternal life, His own life, to us in an act of incredible Love through His Son.

It's been argued that the book of Genesis is just a myth, a story that man created to explain creation and the nature of man and God. It's a book that seems too fantastic to us to be true, too strange to accept as real. If we want to enter the Kingdom of heaven we need to use the currency of heaven—faith—to enter. "In the beginning God" are the first words of the first book of the Bible. If we can't believe in those words, how can we receive the rest of the revelation of the Bible as truth?

We know that faith is the basis of receiving all aspects of salvation—deliverance, health, prosperity, healing, and peace. Throughout the Old Testament we see God revealing His love and His mercy toward us. All He asks us to do is to believe. God made a covenant with Abraham which was a covenant of faith, not of works. *God did not require us to win His favor by good works.* Abraham's blessing became our blessing through covenant. (Rom. 4:16) Covenants are agreements that are kept from generation to generation. They are promises of support, protection, provision, and fellowship. God's covenant to us is eternal.

There are two familiar covenants: The Covenant of Abraham, of faith, and the Mosaic Covenant, of law. The Mosaic Covenant was a covenant of law given to Moses by God as the Hebrews came to the Promised Land. It was a series of laws which, if kept, would earn the favor of God.

Abraham's covenant came long before the Mosaic Law. It was a covenant based solely on faith, not on any earned behaviors. It was the very first covenant God made with us.

Even the Mosaic Law was given to show that faith was what pleased God. The Ten Commandments and all the hundreds of laws that the Mosaic covenant contains are called a "schoolmaster" in the Word. (Gal. 3:24) They showed man that he *cannot earn* his eternal life with the Father. Breaking one law was just as bad as breaking every law; even one sin defiled and separated us from God. The Law could only be fulfilled by living a perfect life.

The only reason God gave us all the laws in the Mosaic covenant was to prove that we need Him, to show that our own good intentions and efforts won't make us good enough, holy enough, or faithful enough to earn a restored relationship and life with Him. He's still the "maker" of our lives. He's still doing all the work (Heb 13:20-21). He gave a free gift of love, in Christ, the love of a Father to His own children.

The Mosaic Covenant taught us that the only way we could be restored to the love and the life of God is through faith in God's love for us. The Abrahamic Covenant was a promise based on faith. That covenant still supersedes the Mosaic Covenant today. (see Heb Chapter 11) And it is fulfilled in Jesus Christ.

Faith was the *only* way that man could receive the blessing of God (Eph 2:8). Religion, defined as keeping laws and traditions that we believe earn God's approval, has always attempted to give us a way to earn the favor of God. It clothes us in guilt, shame, sorrow, and a self-image that demeans us and isolates us from the love and mercy of a wonderful Father. Or it separates us from His mercy by feelings of self-righteousness and self-reliance. Always accusing, never blessing, the power of religion is the power of death (Rom 7:9-11). But the power of relationship in faith and trust is the power of life.

God *is* just and righteous. That is part of our security and assurance in Him. It is why we can trust Him. He is the One who restored us. He is the One who will judge and repay. He is our Defender, our Tower and our Shelter. His Word is sure and we take our peace from it. He is our salvation and His justice is what gives us assurance that what He has provided cannot be taken away (Eph 1:12-14). He's out to get us and return us to our life in Him, not to get us to punish or abuse us. Jesus took that punishment on Himself. That is the love of resurrection. *That is the good news!*

The gospel is the living Word, the Person of Jesus Christ, the Son of God. That Person emptied Himself of His supernatural person. He left His Father, His throne, His heavenly identity and humbled Himself and became a man to fulfill the needs of justice for our sakes (Phil 2:6-8).

He lived the life and paid the price that only a perfect man could pay. He also showed us how to live kind of life that He lived on earth. He walked in the anointing power of the Holy Spirit. That's how He destroyed the yolks of slavery, sickness, and demonic oppression in others. He did that for you, too.

Jesus still reestablishes the life, the peace, the joy, and the "zoe" life of God in us. The power that raised Christ to new life is the same power that raises us to new life (Rom 8:11). That power resides in Christ, and His life can reside in us.

The invitation is always the same, "Come unto me. I am the Way, the Truth, and the Life. No man goes to the Father but by Me. He who believes on Me will have life" (Jn 14:6, Mt 11:28, Jn 3:15). It is the invitation of faith, not of works. *Now that is good news!*

It took more than information to change my life, however. The revelation of Jesus Christ only came after I gave up control over my life to Him. I would like to offer you my personal testimony to bear witness to God's unfailing love and the truth of His Word.

I grew up in the post-war era in a family that did not know how to give or share agape love. As a child I grew up in a family that was essentially "every man for himself." Rejected and abused parents were rejecting and abusing, bound to the woundedness of their own hearts. My own heart resembled theirs. As the years progressed, I was still yearning for intimacy and a sense of self- worth and value.

I felt that love from both of my parents was conditional. That made me rely on my performance and people-pleasing to gain acceptance and favor. I did not develop personal boundaries until much later in my life. The consequence of this was that I could not say "yes" to the good, to the agape love that was offered to me, and I could not say "no" to the bad either. The fruits of this were repeated abusive relationships and addictive behaviors as a young adult. I looked for love in all the wrong places.

The world's spirit kept our father essentially absent as he pursued providing for his family and pursuing his personal goals of success. The acquisition of material goods seemed to be the priority, not bad in itself, but another deception that kept our eyes off the main thing—love, relationship, and intimacy. As my father's daughter, his goals also became mine as I pursued approval and acceptance.

Though my parents rarely attended church, they insisted that my brothers and I attend weekly services. We went alone, without parents or caring adults to guide our spiritual lives. Not feeling the love and acceptance I craved at home, I sought it through religion and obedience to church laws.

But the church could not offer the acceptance, the security, or the celebration my heart longed for. Rejection, condemnation, and performance were my foundations for spiritual growth. Like many religions, the way of the cross was performance and obedience to rules, traditions, and unquestioning faith in the doctrines of the church. But I tried, oh, how I tried! For seventeen years, I put my heart into being the best I could be, but my heart only got more and more bruised.

In that denomination we were discouraged from reading the Bible and admonished to fear the Lord. In those days I pictured God as a stern Father who kept a record of my sins and would make me pay. I believed that His love for me was strictly conditional, and that I could never be sure of eternal security of heaven. Religion only reinforced feelings of alienation, fear, and rejection.

At nineteen, when it was apparent that I had no prospect of mercy there, I sought for a truth that could steer my life without the accompanying fear and condemnation. I studied philosophy and other religions, from the East and the West. I got involved in occult practices, seeking truth. All I found was either dead ends, or worse, demonic torment.

I had had a vision of Jesus when I began my search, but I could not believe that He was here, that is, HERE, for me. I could believe that He was God and that in some mystical way He loved me, but I was still in that performance mode; and I knew that my performance would never earn an intimate relationship with Him. So I went off on my own strength without Him.

I embraced a life of self-service. I lived a life of hidden sin, hidden, because I still wanted to hold on to the persona of purpose, character and integrity. The roller coaster of performance and discouragement, of frenetic work and frenetic play began to have its toll. As one might guess, this double life eventually began breaking down. My life was marred with broken and abusive relationships and a despondency that was overwhelming. My heart was a disaster area.

Success by world standards came but did not hold lasting value to me. The persona lost its allure as the truth of my sorry condition threatened to take my life. I felt abandoned and without resources. The cycle went from bad to worse, and I nearly died of a drug overdose and of other careless activities. All the while I desired to live, but hope had abandoned me either for following God or for steering my own course successfully.

Then, after about fifteen more years of hard living, "suddenlies" started occurring. My dear friend died suddenly. Days later my best friend's baby died from infant death syndrome. I was confronted with my own mortality. Just before her sudden death, my friend, who had recently been "born again," had given me her Bible, all underlined and marked up. I went to it for comfort at her death.

The "suddenlies" continued. Her Bible *spoke* to me! It knew me, spoke to my pain, encouraged me, lifted me, gave me hope, and introduced me to the Father. That Bible was full of a life which eked bit by bit into my heart, my longings, my pain, and my situations. The words of the Bible were my only comfort, and, then, became my only hope.

I had a tutor. I did not know that His name was Holy Spirit, but He spoke to me every time I came to the Bible for a fresh living Word. This was not the God I grew up with. This God was personal, and loving, forgiving, funny, and kind. He offered hope and peace. He offered a life, and I was sorely lacking for one.

It was only a few weeks later that a working companion told me one of the most important things I had ever heard. She spoke to me about GRACE. As soon as I heard it, I *knew* it was the truth. I knew that performance or "works" could not provide a way to eternal security. I had studied too much and tried it all; salvation had to be a free gift by God Himself. *It had to be that simple*.

Grace was the only cup that I could drink. It offered the substance of life. Grace is God's free gift, His mercy and His provision. It is God's favor to me not based on my works but on His Love. All that He had for me was in that cup. That cup is grace.

I found the grace to embrace the life I could not earn, with peace I could not find on earth. Grace brought a joy that I could not sustain myself, and love that I could not earn. It brought provision that I could not achieve on my own. It was the answer to my quest for truth.

For two years I hid myself in that book, afraid of joining a church because I feared that it would try to take from me what I had gained from my relationship with that Book. That Book was the Bible, of course. And the Word of that Book is a Person.

No other book, philosophy, or religion offered that kind

of life, that consistency of power and comfort, that word of promise. I spent all my time in that Word and with that Word. It became my Word, my thought, my plumb line, my standard, my hope and my anchor.

It was the answer. That was the beginning of the walk that has progressively transformed my life.

Now, more than twenty-five years later, grace is still the answer. Grace is still the cup that still brings me what I need. God liberally gives me grace to forgive what or who has wounded me, grace to embrace the unlovely— including myself at times, grace to walk through the fires, grace to climb and then to speak to the mountains. He generously gives me grace to pass the tests and endure the trials. He mercifully gives me grace to enter into the throne room of my Father and to love and be loved unconditionally. Grace—it is a rest; it is a walk. It is God's unmerited favor on and towards me.

Performance has gotten an occasional foothold in my life since then, but then comes the revelation of grace. With great gratitude, I lay down my burdens at the cross of Calvary, repenting for my unbelief and self-reliance, and embrace grace, the yolk of Jesus, my Lord and my Savior.

So now it is apparent. We need the One who wrote the Book, the person of Jesus Christ. To the degree that I will yield myself to Him, I will be filled. "By grace are we saved and not of works. It is the gift of God" (Eph. 2:8).

When the anchor was set and my relationship with God through Jesus Christ was established so that storms could not destroy it, I began to reach out to others and to the Church for relationship. (I don't recommend this as a model; the right church can help establish us in truth and in right relationship. I just happened to be too wounded to trust anyone but Jesus. Even God had to first prove that He would be faithful so that I could trust Him.) I had a lot to learn, and a lot to experience.

I cautiously entered in, following the peace in my heart. I leaned on the Living Word inside me to guide me and to give me revelation, and I have become part of the corporate body of Christ on this earth now. I am still growing and still getting refined, still leaning on and relying on the Spirit of God, my teacher and comforter. I am still abiding in intimate relationship with the triune Living God by grace in love and with a thankful whole heart.

The gospel is good news. It is the *gift* of faith. It is the life of promise. It is the Living Word, Jesus Christ, who has not only provided for our eternal security, but who has also provided for our victory and provision, our peace and joy, our healing and our authority on earth.

Grace brought me more than the assurance of abiding in the kingdom of God in the "sweet by and by." It brought me the very person of Jesus, the Living Word, who embraced my life and now lives in me.

He gave me His life, His mind, and His heart. He gave me His call, His anointing, His Name, and His Nature. The Kingdom of God has come and I have the choice to abide in it here and now. There is love here. There is destiny here. There is peace here. There is promise and a future here. There is power here. There is life here. My identity and my life are now in

Christ. This is the good news of the Gospel of Jesus Christ. It *has* the power to transform lives. The good news is that the kingdom of God has come. We can abide in it now and receive its blessings *now*, by faith in Jesus Christ. I call that good news!

RELATED SCRIPTURES (KJV)

John 1:17 For the law was given by Moses, but grace and truth came by Jesus Christ.

Luke 7:50 And he said to the woman, Thy faith hath saved thee; go in peace.

John 3:17 For God sent not his Son into the world to condemn the world; but that the world through him might be saved.

John 10:9-10 I am the door: by me if any man enter in, he shall be saved, and shall go in and out, and find pasture. The thief cometh not, but for to steal, and to kill, and to destroy: I am come that they might have life, and that they might have it more abundantly.

Acts 2:21 And it shall come to pass, that whosoever shall call on the name of the Lord shall be saved.

Acts 4:12 Neither is there salvation in any other: for there is none other name under heaven given among men, whereby we must be saved.

Rom 5:10-12 For if, when we were enemies, we were reconciled to God by the death of his Son, much more, being reconciled, we shall be saved by his life. And not only so, but we also joy in God through our Lord Jesus Christ, by whom we have now received the atonement. Wherefore, as by one man sin entered into the world, and death by sin; and so death passed upon all men, for that all have sinned:

Rom 10:9 That if thou shalt confess with thy mouth the Lord Jesus, and shalt believe in thine heart that God hath raised him from the dead, thou shalt be saved.

1 Cor 1:18 For the preaching of the cross is to them that perish foolishness: but unto us which are saved it is the power of God.

Eph 2:5 Even when we were dead in sins, hath quickened us together with Christ. (by grace ye are saved;)

Eph 2:8-9 For by grace are ye saved through faith; and that not of yourselves: it is the gift of God: Not of works, lest any man should boast.

1 Tim 2:3-6 For this is good and acceptable in the sight of God our Saviour; Who will have all men to be saved, and to come unto the knowledge of the truth. For there is one God, and one mediator between God and men, the man Christ Jesus; Who gave himself a ransom for all, to be testified in due time.

2 Tim 1:9 Who hath saved us, and called us with an holy calling, not according to our works, but according to his own purpose and grace, which was given us in Christ Jesus before the world began.

Titus 3:5-6 Not by works of righteousness which we have done, but according to his mercy he saved us, by the washing of regeneration, and renewing of the Holy Ghost; Which he shed on us abundantly through Jesus Christ our Saviour;

A PRAYER OF INVITATION

TO THE LORD, JESUS CHRIST

Jesus, I believe with my heart that You are the Son of God. I believe You died for me, paid the price for my sin, and that You rose for me. Wash me in Your precious blood and cleanse me of all my sin. Your grace alone has saved me. I confess with my mouth that You, Jesus, are my Lord and my Savior. I make the great exchange. I give you my heart and receive yours. Thank you for transforming my life. I believe.

What shall separate us

from the love of Christ?

Shall tribulation, or distress,

or persecution, or famine,

or nakedness, or peril, or sword?

As it is written, For thy sake we are killed all the day long; we

are accounted as sheep for the slaughter. Nay, in all these things

we are more than conquerors through him that loved us.

For I am persuaded,

that neither death,

nor life, nor angels,

nor principalities, nor powers,

nor things present,

nor things to come,

nor height, nor depth,

nor any other creature,

shall be able to separate us

from the love of God,

which is in Christ Jesus our Lord.

(Rom 8:35-39 KJV)

**On the fifth day of Christness
my Lord, He gave to me**

FIVE SIGNS AND WONDERS

And these signs shall follow them that
believe:

In my name shall they cast out devils;

they shall speak with new tongues;

they shall take up serpents;

and if they drink any deadly thing,
                it shall not hurt them;

they shall lay hands on the sick,
                and they shall recover.

Mark 16:17-18 (KJV)

Signs and wonders have not ceased;

God is still alive and well,
Ruling and reigning
By the authority of His body,
The Church--
Born again sons and daughters of the Father,
Believers
Who walk in the Spirit,
Love the unlovely,
And fulfill the Great Commission
With faith
And expectation
That the Word of God is true.

Do signs and wonders follow you?

Some believers and denominational, traditional churches question about the manifestation of signs and wonders in the church today. Some believe that the days of miracles has ceased, that miracles witnessed in the Gospels and the Book of Acts were for a time past. Still others believe that miracles today are random acts of God perhaps based on our "goodness" or just deserts, or perhaps, simply a matter of "luck."

But let us ask ourselves these questions: Has God changed? Is the Word of God living and true? Is God's love really unconditional? Are His promises true all the time, or just part of the time? Is the Holy Spirit really abiding in us just as He did in Jesus? What empowered the disciples and those others to do the works of Jesus? Are we any different from them?

Well, we know that God does not change, and that He is faithful and true (James 1:17). We know in our believing heart that God's Word is alive because Jesus Christ has resurrected and sits at the right hand of the Father (Heb. 10:12). We know that God's Testament is His promise, and that He cannot lie (1 Sam. 15:29). We also know that God is no respecter of persons, that what He has done for one, He shall do for others (Col. 3:25). We know by the inner witness in our heart that the same Spirit that raised Christ from the grave resides in us (Rom. 8:11). We know that the Word of God is God-breathed and cannot err. We know these truths because we believe the in the inerrancy of the Bible (2 Tim. 3:16).

Don't we? If there is any question of these basic tenants of Bible-believing New Testament Christians, then perhaps we should go back to the milk of the Word and examine our beliefs. Without faith it is impossible to please God (Heb. 11:6).

Jesus said that the works that He did we would do also, that is, we, His disciples (John 14:12). In His Name we would see signs and wonders accompany His Word to confirm His truth (1 Cor. 2:4, 5, 20; Heb. 2:3-4).

Let's assume we are in agreement with all this. I am aware that this assumption is a big leap of faith for some readers. The same faith that saves us is the same faith that heals us. The atonement was a complete work (Isa. 53). The same Holy Spirit Who guides us is the same Holy Spirit Who manifests God's glory to and through us. The same Holy Spirit Who manifested as tongues of fire over the disciples in the upper room on Pentecost, Who spoke through the believers with new tongues (spiritual languages), and Who healed the sick and raised the dead through the apostles is the same Holy Spirit Who abides in us. God says He is no respecter of persons (Acts 10:34). He also says that He does not change (Mal. 3:6).

An examination of the revivals of the last hundred years alone will attest to the miracle-working power that accompanies the preaching of the Gospel. Evan Roberts, Alexander Dowie, John G. Lake, Smith Wigglesworth, Marie Woodworth Etter, Aimee Semple McPherson, A. A. Allen, and Kathryn Khulman are some recent historical preachers and evangelists whose ministries were accompanied by signs and wonders. Miraculous healings were common in their meetings. People experienced a touch of God in a very tangible way, and their lives were forever changed. The vessels God used to bring His gifts were by no means perfect people. They were, however, "sold out" to Jesus. They focused on the supernatural realities rather than the mere natural circumstances around them. They shared deep intimacy with God through the Holy Spirit. They knew God personally, and they had learned how to hear His voice and respond to His Word. They were able to bring that Word to those who sought help or wanted to know this God themselves.

More recently T. L. Osborne, Reinhard Bonnke, Benny Hinn, Benson Idahosa, Ruth Heflin, David Hogan, Heidi Baker, Randy Clark, Bill Johnson and a host of others, some famous, and most not, have witnessed the moves of God which have brought countless believers to the cross of Christ. Like those who came before them, they learned how to walk with God, hear His voice, and respond to His presence. They are "carriers" of God's glory, able to transmit that glory so that others can experience the touch of God that they crave. They are not perfect people, either. But they knew the Word, the Living Word, Jesus, and they share intimacy through the Holy Spirit with the Father. They believed the promises, and press in to receive and to share them with others. The life of Christ in them manifests through them in the power of God's love. Perhaps now, we can accept that God will honor the preaching of His Word with signs and wonders following. This is the promise of His Word (Mk 16:20).

So, what's the problem? Why aren't we seeing God's word confirmed by more people of faith in Christ? Do they have something we don't have?

I believe the answer is "yes and no." Yes, they do have something—that thing I call "*Christness*," the state or condition of Christ in us. These mountain-movers and world-shakers have a personal revelation and outpouring of the Living Word that they received by renewing their minds and hearts to the things of God.

That revelation came as a result of seeking God's presence by meditation of the Word and by prayer and the exercise of their faith and by staying hungry and open for the "zoe" of God. The result is a transformation of the mind, that is, being more mindful and believing of the things of God than of the things of man and his natural worldview.

Compared to some other world cultures, we of the Western world have a harder time to believe in our heart what our minds can't readily accept as true. But the mind can only accept as true that which the heart believes!

In order to flow in the gifts of the Spirit, including miracles, we must walk in the mind of Christ so that the words of Christ will speak through us. Then the works of Christ will manifest through us.

These miracle workers are moved by the same compassion and love that characterized Jesus Christ in His earthly ministry. His heart has become their heart. These devil chasers walk by faith not by sight. Their yielded hearts remain always hungry for the presence of God. These good news bringers are people of action who confidently speak out the creative Word of God in expectation and utter reliance upon the Holy Spirit to fulfill and complete the Word of God. Sensitive to the Holy Spirit, these believers are following the lead of the Spirit, hearing the heart of the Father, and moving in the faith of Christ.

When we are recreated in Christ, we are also endowed with His mind (1 Cor. 2:16). But just as we drink milk as babies, and grow to become mature, so, too, we are responsible for the growth and maturity of the mind of Christ in us. "Be not conformed to this world, but be ye transformed by the renewing of your mind that you may prove what is the perfect and acceptable will of God" (Rom 12:2).

The mind of Christ is supernatural. We must not limit ourselves with our natural mind. In fact, we *cannot* limit ourselves to the realm of sensory data, the natural world-system man. Miracles are birthed in the realm of the supernatural, the realm of the Spirit. They exist in the realm of the glory of the living God.

Jesus was the Anointed One in 100-fold measure. It is literally Christ and His Anointing that now abides in us (1 John 2:27). Our faith should stand in the power of God who is not only above us, but is also *within* and *upon* us (1 Cor. 2:5).

To walk in the realm of miracles, we cannot rely on the wisdom of men. We cannot rely on tradition, the faith of our fathers, upon any other person's faith, or even a personal, past experience. The anointing of God needs to be received afresh each day. It is the "living bread" (John 6:51) that feeds, the "fresh oil" (Ps 92:10) that brings in the "new thing" (Is 43:19).

The anointing is the power of God. In order for that anointing to flow through us, the Word tells us to stir up the gift in us (2 Tim. 1:6). In worship, in prayer and meditation in the Word, in fasting and faith, through intimacy in the presence of God, the gift of God, the Holy Spirit will arise in us. The Holy Spirit can only anoint us to be like Jesus after we have come to the place of revelation, of *rhema* (personally received in our heart as the God-breathed word of faith) understanding. Then we will respond just as we saw Jesus in His own earthly ministry. As we speak in faith, the power will come with the authority of the Name of Jesus. That is how those great revivalists moved in signs and wonders. That is how we, too, can walk.

With a transformation of the mind, being more mindful of the realm of the Kingdom of God than of our own simple kingdom ruled by our senses and time and space, miracles become commonplace, for they exist in the Kingdom of God for us. Jesus told the disciples to tell the people that the *Kingdom of God has come!* We need the miracles *now;* we need healing and wholeness and provision *now*; we need a touch of God *now*. And it is ours, available to us, *now*, in the Kingdom of God.

Miracles are a manifestation of God's love and compassion for us. They are the promises of God manifesting by the love of God in the transformed heart—yours and mine—to us and through us, to others.

These ministers are no more special than you or I. God will do the same through you as He does or did through them. Signs and wonders are not a matter only of dispensation, but of revelation. It is surely a matter of faith.

We are literally transformed by a revelation from God. We *change*; literally, we are *transformed.* Like the Word says, the old things pass away and behold! everything is new. Let me share some of the signs and wonders that God has so liberally poured into my own life.

As I read the Bible in my first God encounters I found peace, rest, then hope, and then, joy. That was a sign and a wonder to me! I grew confident in God, and learned to trust Him. That was a very big issue for me, and it did not occur overnight. It was the Lord Himself in the inner voice of the Holy Spirit through the Word of the Bible who convinced me.

When I had a revelation that God my Father loved me unconditionally, I *changed*; I was *transformed*. I didn't fear coming to God in prayer; now I wanted to charge into His throne room to thank Him and love on Him and let Him love on me. I became secure in my relationship with Him. It was not a relationship based on my performance or good works, but only on my acceptance of His marvelous grace and love for me. That trust is another sign and wonder!

When I had the revelation that by the stripes of Jesus I was healed, I was *changed*. Pain left my body and health replaced weakness. Sometimes it was "all of a sudden," and sometimes it came more gradually. But it has always come. Now, even in times of "bad reports," I cling to the FACT that my redeemer lives and that His word, His report is the truth I cling to. I believe in God's healing miracles.

Even when threatened with death, my confidence in God's healing promise was greater than my confidence in my symptoms and situation. I couldn't be lured away from the truth I knew in my heart. That truth was more than a word. He was, and is, a Person, committed to me and to His Word. "Christ in you, the hope of glory" (Col 1:27).

When I had the revelation that I had authority over wickedness in my life, I *changed.* I wasn't afraid of the devil. I began to talk to him the same way Jesus did, in faith. I slept better; depression didn't rule me; fear didn't have its way. Now I could begin to recognize the lies that were literally determining my attitudes about me and my potential. A renewed mind is another sign and wonder I so cherish!

I had the power and authority to stop the lie from influencing my decisions and my heart feelings. The Bible says to resist the devil and he shall surely flee from you (James 4:7). Once I started to recognize the truth, that is, the way God sees things, including me, and believe what He has to say about them and me, everything in my life began to change. Friends even noticed a change in my appearance. Some asked if I was in love! I had to tell them about Jesus!

When I discovered that my mind was operating in the darkness of judgments and bitter root expectations, the love and life of Christ in me gave me the power to literally make my mind new, and exchange the lies that bound me for the Truth that let me be free to love myself and others like Father loves. This kind of love is a sign and wonder! This new compassion and mercy is a sign and a wonder!

As I matured in Christ new challenges came, challenges that stretched my faith and my capacity to drink in the presence and the love of God. My part was to stay in the refiner's fire and to trust God. My part was to allow God to root out the old mind sets and beliefs that kept me treading around that mountain yet another time. Each new revelation comes with a challenge of faith. But each challenge carries with it the grace to walk it through and to come out in victory.

All these *changes* are signs and wonders to me! I could not make any of this happen by my own ability or wishful thinking. Positive thinking didn't heal me, restore me, or complete me. God did all the work as I let go of the lies, the bitterness, and the bondages that held me back. *I am a sign and a wonder*! The first miracle is the miracle of salvation, the gift of God by grace not works. Now God works *through* me as He pours His goodness to others.

Doubt or unbelief and reliance on the "tried and true" suppresses and the arrests miracle working power of God in our lives. Paul's preaching was a good example of the operating process of the working of miracles. He preaching was "not with enticing words and wisdom of men, but in power and demonstration of the spirit" so that our faith "should not stand in the wisdom of men, but in the power of God" (1 Cor. 2:4-5).

His life after his rebirth in Christ is a model to us. Paul's life was dominated by faith. He knew the word not only by study but by personal revelation by the Spirit of God. His encounter with the Lord radically changed every aspect of His life. When he came to the revelation of Christ in him, he says he did not even condemn himself for his past, because God didn't! He was totally sold out to manifest and live the life of Christ in him. He was committed to a purpose. He was utterly dependent upon the Holy Spirit and the anointing for every aspect of his ministry to others and to God. And God used him to pen His revelation to believers in epistles we find in the New Testament.

The Holy Spirit will also develop in us the kind of power that is more than our ability to ask, think, or imagine. The might that flows out of us comes from the seed that was planted and nurtured and, then, matured by the Holy Spirit when we were recreated in Christ.

It's so easy to fall into the trap of thinking that we must do or be something by our own efforts and abilities to earn God's approval. As we grow in Christ, God our Father trains and disciplines our hearts and minds, as a good parent with unconditional love always at the fore. He can't love us any more...or less. As we grow in *Christness*, we learn the pleasure of service and the responsibility of obedience with a willing and open, trusting heart.

When Jesus Christ was raised to become King of Kings and Lord of Lords, He also became a father. Sitting at the right hand with our Abba Father, Jesus is always making intercession for us, watching over us, providing and empowering us, making a way for us to come into the fullness of His life in us. He has created a kingdom for us, and it's His utmost desire for us to have it all.

When we receive a revelation of God, our minds are transformed, our hearts are empowered, and we become like Christ in that revelation. You've probably heard the saying, "You can't give what you don't have." That saying is true! We can only give out that revelation of Jesus Christ that has become a part of you. It starts small, but builds as we continue to grow in

Christness.

Maybe for you it started with being able to give joy by sharing your encounter with God. Then as Christ in you manifested, you were able to give faith and hope and unconditional love. Perhaps your words of wisdom or knowledge revealed God's love to someone that changed their life. The joy for us is that as we give what we have been so freely given, our own hearts expand and we receive even *more* of the life of God in us! What hope! What confidence! What promise!

Like Christ, what I have received freely, I freely give. I have become a "hose" for God. He can pour out His life, His anointing, through me. I am His vessel; it is His love, His healing, His peace, His promise, His life that I am delivering. What He's done *to* me now He does *through* me.

The same anointing that manifested through Jesus Christ by the power of the Holy Spirit abides in you and in me, the born-again disciples of Jesus Christ. The magnitude of its manifestation is generally up to us. Though God can move sovereignly, that is, independent of our will, He rarely does. We are His body on earth, His vessel, His hands, His love reaching out to the lost, the hurting, and the hungry. He told his disciples that we who believe in Him would do greater works than He because He was going to the Father (Jn 14:12).

Signs and wonders are the confirmation that God's Word is true, and that He will back up His Word with His Power. His motivation is love. His desire is intimacy with His children. Signs and wonders are the outpouring of the love of God wooing in the prodigal son and daughter, fulfilling the heart desires of the yearning soul.

There's a fresh outpouring of God's Spirit on the earth today. It is the Spirit of love and of power. It is the same kind of Spirit that we read about in the book of Acts. The supernatural will become more commonplace, natural. You will see it on the streets, in parking lots, homes, and other "unlikely" places! And He is using people like you and me!

God is calling each one of us to come to the fullness of His life in us. That means that we will have to, like Peter, "get out of the boat" of our traditions and old ways that made us feel secure, so that we could be and do what we couldn't before. Peter walked on the water, just like Jesus, until self-consciousness with its natural limitations overtook him. But Peter didn't drown because Jesus was there to lift him up. They walked back to the boat on the water together! Jesus told Pete to just keep the faith!

God put His life in you. He's given you His Holy Spirit indwelling in you. The promise is for greater things, but we need to accept that for ourselves and begin to act like the promise is true and for us, not just for a few special people, for the delegated clergy, our pastors or evangelists. The five-fold ministry described in Ephesians—apostles, pastors, evangelists, prophets, and teachers—are not the people called to do the greater works; they are the ones called to train up and equip the body of Christ, the Church to do the greater works!

This is the day of the Saints, the *Christed* ones, to manifest the life of Jesus Christ in their everyday walks. It's the day, the season, we have been seeking, the one that has been spoken of in Joel, Ezra, Daniel, Ezekiel and other books of the Old and New Testaments. Signs and wonders will be the visible demonstration of the love and power of God in Christ to meet the needs and the heart's desires of His beloved.

In His Name, now our authority by legal right, in unwavering faith, and in the compassion of Jesus Christ, whose body on earth we now are, we shall do the works of our Lord. His signs and wonders shall confirm the Word on our lips. That is the God kind of faith. That is the God kind of living. That is the promise of God. This is the promise for you!

Truly, truly, I say to you, he who believes in Me, the works that I do shall he do also; and greater works than these shall he do; because I go to the Father. And whatever you ask in My name, that will I do, that the Father may be glorified in the Son.

(John 14:12-13 NASB)

RELATED SCRIPTURES (KJV)

Heb 2:3-4 How shall we escape, if we neglect so great salvation; which at the first began to be spoken by the Lord, and was confirmed unto us by them that heard him; God also bearing them witness, both with signs and wonders, and with divers miracles, and gifts of the Holy Ghost, according to his own will?

Mark 16:20 And they went forth, and preached every where, the Lord working with them, and confirming the word with signs following. Amen.

Luke 10:19 Behold, I give unto you power to tread on serpents and scorpions, and over all the power of the enemy: and nothing shall by any means hurt you.

Luke 24:49 And, behold, I send the promise of my Father upon you: but tarry ye in the city of Jerusalem, until ye be endued with power from on high.

Acts 1:8 But ye shall receive power, after that the Holy Ghost is come upon you: and ye shall be witnesses unto me both in Jerusalem, and in all Judaea, and in Samaria, and unto the uttermost part of the earth.

Acts 5:12 And by the hands of the apostles were many signs and wonders wrought among the people; and they were all with one accord in Solomon's porch.

1 Cor 1:24 But unto them which are called, both Jews and Greeks, Christ the power of God, and the wisdom of God.

1 Cor 2:4-5 And my speech and my preaching was not with enticing words of man's wisdom, but in demonstration of the Spirit and of power: That your faith should not stand in the wisdom of men, but in the power of God.

1 Cor 4:20 For the kingdom of God is not in word, but in power.

2 Cor 4:7 But we have this treasure in earthen vessels, that the excellency of the power may be of God, and not of us.

Eph 1:19-20 And what is the exceeding greatness of his power to us-ward who believe, according to the working of his mighty power, Which he wrought in Christ, when he raised him from the dead, and set him at his own right hand in the heavenly places,

1 Th 1:5 For our gospel came not unto you in word only, but also in power, and in the Holy Ghost, and in much assurance; as ye know what manner of men we were among you for your sake.

2 Tim 1:7 For God hath not given us the spirit of fear; but of power, and of love, and of a sound mind.

2 Tim 3:2-5 For men shall be lovers of their own selves, covetous, boasters, proud, blasphemers, disobedient to parents, unthankful, unholy, Without natural affection, trucebreakers, false accusers, incontinent, fierce, despisers of those that are good, Traitors, heady, highminded, lovers of pleasures more than lovers of God; Having a form of godliness, but denying the power thereof: from such turn away.

1 Cor 12:7 But the manifestation of the Spirit is given to every man to profit withal.

On the sixth day of Christness,
my Lord, He gave to me

SIX PIECES OF ARMOR

Put on the whole armor of God that ye may be able to **stand** against the wiles of the devil.

For **we wrestle not against flesh and blood**, but against principalities, against powers, against the rulers of the darkness of this world, against spiritual wickedness in high places.

Wherefore take unto you the whole armor of God that ye may be able to withstand in the evil day, and having done all, to stand.

Stand therefore, having your loins girt about with **truth,** and having on the breastplate of **righteousness;**

And your feet shod with the preparation of the gospel of **peace;**

Above all, taking the shield of **faith,** wherewith ye shall be able to quench all the fiery darts of the wicked.

And take the helmet of **salvation,** and the sword of the Spirit, which is the **word of God**:

Praying always with all prayer and supplication in the Spirit, and watching thereunto with all perseverance and supplication for all saints;

Ephesians 6:11-18 (KJV) [emphasis, mine]

There are Always Giants to Slay!

When Abraham answered God's call,
Giants planned then for his fall;
Fear and need he had to face,
But God provided help and grace.

David fought a grizzly bear,
And then a lion with golden hair.
With five smooth stones in his bare hand
He slew five giants in that bad land!

Esther, queen, with beauty fair,
Set a table and then a lair,
To capture Haman in his vain plot
To kill her people, but killed he got!

Jesus on the cross he cried
"It is finished!" and then he died;
And as he rose in victory
He displayed our vanquished enemy.

You're in the army of the Lord!
You won't perish by the enemy's sword.
Wear your armor, tried and true,
God's victory now lives in you!

Not by might, not by power, but by my Spirit says the
Lord (Zech 4:6).

The verse that precedes this is one of the keys to understanding this passage. Ephesians 6:10 says, "Finally, my brethren, be strong in the Lord, and in the power of his might." Our strength comes not from our own physical prowess, not from our achievements, our family heritage, nor any other thing on this earth. God is not impressed with our personal mortal or moral strength. He is moved by our faith in Him, on our reliance of His Words in our heart and on our mouth.

What pleases God is, simply, God. When God sees in us the God-kind of faith, He is pleased and He responds because He always honors His Word.

The Bible tells us that it is not by might or by power that we have the victory, but by the Spirit of the Lord (Zech. 4:6). In another passage, the Word says that the joy of the Lord is our strength (Neh. 8:10), and in another we are told to *put on* our strength (Isa. 52:1).

Obviously, the kind of power and strength that the Bible is referring to has a divine origin. It is not physical ability, mental achievement, or willful determination. In fact, there is no mention *at all* of our own personal abilities or natural attributes!

The same passage (Isa. 52:1) calls our strength "beautiful garments." Strongs's *Concordance* translates this as robes of majesty and honor. The character of Jesus Christ is more than a learned behavior. Character is developed through perseverance in hard times. Character is tested and tried. The character of Christ is the life and heart of the Son of God manifested in our homes, our relationships, in every part of our lives.

We are told to put on the whole armor of God so that we will be *able* to stand against the wiles of the devil. Our battle is *not* with human beings, with physical circumstances, or with the natural elements. To the natural mind, this sounds like nonsense. And so it should. "The man without the Spirit does not accept the things that come from the Spirit of God, for they are foolishness to him, and he cannot understand them, because they are spiritually discerned" (1 Cor. 2:14 NIV). The foolishness of God is wiser than men; and the weakness of God is stronger than men (1 Cor 1:25).

If the battle is not with the people who wound us, with the circumstances that stress us out, or with the natural elements that hinder or harm us, then we need to get a revelation of who or what we are battling.

Can we be attacked by something we can't see with our natural eye? Of course. We can't see bacteria or a virus, yet they can destroy a human life. We can't see electricity, but it can do some serious damage to our bodies if we connect with it. We can't see words, yet they have the power to break our hearts, our spirit, and our resolve.

We have a sworn enemy. He is the same enemy who got the lease of the earth from the first Adam, and who dwells through principalities over the earth. In the Bible he has many names, among which are the accuser (Rev 12:10), the thief (Jn 10:10), the destroyer (Rev 9:11), adversary (1 Pet 5:8), prince of this world (1 Jn 12:31-32), and the antichrist (1Jn 4:3). He is the same enemy that crucified Christ. He is the same enemy whom Christ defeated at the cross.

A principality, or "pal," is an area of dominion in the heavenlies. When one-third of the angels fell and were cast out of the presence of God, they were cast onto the domain of the earth. They have a lease on the earth because of the sin of Adam and Eve. We are taking back our promised land when we fight the good fight of faith, and Jesus Himself will complete the work when He returns to claim His full inheritance!

Ephesians 6 tells us that we wrestle "against principalities, against powers, against the rulers of the darkness of this world, against spiritual wickedness in high places." How? You stand!

The word, "stand," is more than a physical act. According to Strong's *Concordance* (Strongs G2476), "stand" means to abide, appoint, bring, continue, covenant, establish, hold up, lay, present, set (up), stanch, stand (by, forth, still, up). Interestingly, the cross reference in the definition describes this word as in a passive or horizontal posture and different from another form which means in an active or upright position (Strongs G5087).

It would appear that "stand" has the opposite meaning than we would naturally ascribe to it. "Standing" here means abiding, or residing in the *rest* and confidence of our covenant with God. We are lead and kept by God's peace.

Abiding in Him, I am established by divine covenant. Our Father has given us a covenant of peace by both the Abrahamic covenant and the New Covenant in Christ. He has promised us protection, provision, and rest. In Christ, we are established in that covenant; we are positioned, placed, and settled. The battle is the Lord's.

Resting in His promise, I am not standing in my own strength; it would avail nothing anyway. I am standing on the rock (Jesus) of my faith. I know that God keeps His promises to me, that His covenant with me is sure. I stand in faith in Him. The scripture shows me how to stand, or abide in Christ.

We are told to put on armor. That doesn't sound like rest or peace to the natural mind. That sounds like battle. And it is. Enforcing peace in our hearts, resting in the covenant promise, relying on God, our Father, to hasten to perform His Word *is* a battle. We must cast down every vain imagination, as Paul says, every thought that does not abide in the peace and rest of God (2 Cor 10:5).

This task is not easy in the adverse circumstances of our lives. We need to be encouraged, strengthened, and even supported by the power and love of the Holy Spirit in us and through the body of Christ. We are a part of an army. We are not "lone rangers." Our reward is coming if we do not lose heart. Let us examine a few examples of putting on the armor of God in the Old Testament, for it is our schoolmaster.

When God led the Hebrews to the Promised Land, Moses sent out scouts to see what lay ahead. Ten of the twelve brought back negative reports, saying that giants were there and that the Israelites were as grasshoppers compared to them. Only two brought back good reports. They were the only two of those twelve to enter into that Promised Land. We see here that confession plays an important part in possessing the promises of God.

The Jews had to take the land that God had promised them. They lacked the battlements, the weapons, the manpower, the strategy, and the expertise of their enemy. But they had something none of the giants had: they had Jehova God.

In every battle, God provided strategy, power, and even reinforcements! In every battle, the victory was accomplished by reliance upon God, by obedience to His lead, and by divine execution. The first battle took place at Jericho.

At Jericho the people, led by priests and dancers, armed with praise and worship, tambourines and trumpets, marched around a city for seven days in silence. Then on the seventh day the priests blew the trumpets and the people shouted, and the walls of the city fell down flat. The inhabitants fled, and the Israelites took the territory (Josh 5:13-6-27). Archeological findings have offered historical evidence to support the sudden tumbling of the wall. It was a wall so thick that chariots raced on top. God fought the battle for His children. The Promised Land became theirs. But the battles were not over. There were still other giants in the land!

In the war against the Amalekites, Joshua with his troops were winning the battle as long as Moses, who stood afar off on a mountain top, kept his arms up in prayer. When Moses' arms fell, the battle below went against the Hebrews. Two men came to help Moses, holding up his arms, and putting a rock under his head. Joshua, in the heat of the battle, thought he needed new strategies as the enemy overtook them, but his victory had nothing to do with his actions. His victory was a consequence of Moses calling upon the Name of the Lord continually (Exo 17:10-16). The Promised Land became theirs.

When Debra and Barak went against the enemy to reclaim Mt. Tabor, the Israelites had no weapons. But in obedience to God, they took ten thousand men and marched against an army with countless soldiers with powerful weapons. God sent hailstorms and the Bible says the earth trembled. The enemy in confusion and fear was utterly defeated (2 Judges, 4-5). That Promised Land became theirs.

The Old Testament shows us that reliance on God is the key to our victory. We do not wrestle against flesh and blood; people are not our problem. The root is in spiritual places. It is here that we must battle the real enemy.

"And all this assembly shall know that the LORD saveth not with sword and spear: for the battle is the Lord's" (1 Sam 17:47). Our part is to put on our armor, exercise the authority given to us by Christ, declare the Word of God upon our situations, and stand in faith.

We need spiritual armor to win the battles in our earthly life. The Bible tells us what that armor is: salvation, righteousness, the Word of God, peace, truth, and faith surrounded by and saturated in prayer in the Spirit.

Now we know that successful business people have learned to dress for success. It is no secret that our presentation is important. To win a championship fight, we must be convinced that we have already won before we enter the ring. Motivational speakers tell us that if we don't envision ourselves as winning the race, it is very unlikely that we ever shall. The Bible says that without a vision, the people perish (Prov. 29:18).

The big difference between humanistic thinking and Christianity is that we Christians know that it is by His might, not ours, that we have the victory (Zec 4:6). For a Christian, believing is seeing. A Christian will not rob God of His glory.

The words we speak have creative power because we are created in God's image. God honors His Word with action. We speak God's promises from the Bible out of the *Christed* renewed mind, minds that understand and abide in our true identity and authority. Motivated by the God-kind-of-love, we speak with the God-kind-of-faith. Relying in Him to perform His word, we live in expectation and assurance of the outcome in peace and rest (Heb 11:1).

The armor of God is tangible, because it does indeed have substance, but it is the substance of *character* that we are striving to put on. That character is the same character of Jesus Christ. Jesus *is* our armor. By looking at each part described we can begin to get an idea of how the character of Jesus Christ in us is the path to our victory in every battle of our life.

The "helmet of salvation" covers our head. It is an outward sign of an inward transformation. Jesus Christ is the head of the body, the church (Ps 140:7). He is our head. The helmet of salvation covers the head, which is the decision-making part of our body. In Christ, we have the mind of Christ (1 Cor 2:16). Relying on Him, we receive the strategies for success. Like the saints of the Old Testament, we can rely on God's plan. Our reliance and obedience to it delivers to us our promised land.

A helmet is not transparent. The enemy cannot read our minds. He can only know and act on the words that come from our mouth! So we have to guard our tongues, being careful of what we confess to be true! Our words become an open door for things to come upon us. Our words have power. They are the doors to our heart! Not only must we renew our minds to the mind of Christ, but then we need to put a guard on our tongues so that we don't say things that may open doors to our own or another's harm or destruction.

In *Christness*, we abide with God in the secret place (Ps. 91). Our old mindset of self-reliance, dead philosophy, and selfish gain has been replaced by the Word of God. Every arena of our life, including health, finance, relationship, and desire, are subject to His ways now. Relying on Him, we receive His strategy as well as His direction and promises. That is our confidence.

Our minds are now being transformed to the mind of Christ. Don't be discouraged if the Word you speak does not come to pass immediately. Faith's partner, patience, will have her perfect work, too (Heb. 6:12). Just don't lose heart.

The "breastplate of righteousness" covers our heart and our lungs. Our hearts are right with God as we abide in Christ. We are in right standing with our Father, and we have the boldness and the security to know that we can come to Him with our heart's need. The blood of Christ has removed all stain of sin from us, and we know that we are fully accepted and unconditionally loved by our Father. Our heart is undivided, whole, and we can live in the peace of His love. We know that our inheritance is sure, and we can breathe easy. Christ has become our righteousness.

Our lungs are filled with the breath of God, for it is in Him that we live and move and have our being. The Holy Spirit Himself abides in us. He is our comforter, teacher, and guide. He not only seals our inheritance and position in Christ, He also manifests the life of God in and through our lives, revealing the righteousness that we have been given freely through Christ.

The breath of God is the power of God, the same breath that brought Adam and Eve to life. The breath of God, the Holy Spirit, brings us revelation that leads to greater intimacy with Jesus and our Father. Knowing whose we are helps us to know who we are. Knowing who we are secures and empowers us. We breathe freely of the fragrance of heaven on earth in us.

Around our loins is a "girdle of truth." Loins speak of strength. Our loins also shield the reproductive organs of our body. Jesus is the Way, the Truth, and the Life (Jn 14:6). He is our strength and the giver of life. This piece of armor is an outward sign that the seed of God, planted in us is vital and life-producing. That life is the life of the Spirit, of the Kingdom of God. We are not deceived by the spirit of the world or by powers and principalities of the enemy. Truth, Jesus Christ, gives us His strength to take Spirit-directed action to achieve victory.

Our feet are "shod with the preparation of the gospel of peace." That means we are led by peace, not by need. Our motivation is our Father's motivation: love and faith in peace. We are no longer motivated by need, fear, want, or by our circumstances. We do not make haste when trials and tribulation come upon us. Rather, we seek the guidance of the Holy Spirit, and when we have His peace in our hearts, we move in the direction that His peace dictates. Since God supplies all our needs, we are not distressed or anxious about how we shall live. We respond with obedience in faith to the direction of God. He will keep us in peace through all the circumstances of our life. This is more than an ideal; it is the Reality. The challenge is to enforce it in the midst of fearful circumstances!

Christ is our shield. He is our protector and defender. He is the Commander-in-Chief of the Lord's army, and He fights our battles for us. Our part is to exercise the God-kind-of-faith, the faith that quells all the "darts," the evils that come to rob and destroy us. As we keep our focus on Him, in dependency and faith, Christ literally shields our hearts, our souls, and our lives and takes the hit for us. He did that at the cross for everyone.

The peace of God needs to be practiced. We do that by renewing our minds by the love of the Holy Spirit and to the Word of God. We also want to purge our hearts of anything that is working against us.

Judgments are like stakes in our heart that keep us bound to the hurt and the bitterness of a wounding. We can only be free of that memory and its fruit when we forgive and release the judgments we made against the wounder or the wounding. Then our hearts are free.

We may need to enter into His gates when we find ourselves outside of His peace through thanksgiving and worship. We may need to come through the portal of a broken heart, repenting for missing the mark of His goodness and love, for relying on ourselves and wounding ourselves or others in the fray.

Continue to press in to the peace of God until it envelops us in rest and trust in God. When our hearts are one with the Father, He can respond to our requests.

He is teaching us to walk by faith and agape love, the kind of love that lives to give and knows how to receive, too. His peace is also the calling card that draws a lost and hurting person to the love and salvation of a wonderful Savior.

Walking in the character of Christ, we share the good news of what Christ has done for us. We approach others through the peace of God in our hearts. We do not engage in doctrinal argument; it is not our job to prove anything to anyone (2Tim 2:14). As ambassadors of love, we come to share the peace, the joy, the promises, and the very life of Christ. We believe that it is God who calls, God who begins the work of salvation, and God who finishes the work in a person's heart (Heb 12:2). We don't need to help Him!

Jesus' calling card is also ours. He loves the sinner and hates the sin. He heals the sick and the lame and heals the broken hearted. He delivers the tormented soul from the devils that bind them. He forgives sin and rebukes hypocrisy. This has become our mission, too, our calling card, too.

Jesus Christ is our armor. He is peace; He is truth; He is salvation; He is righteousness; He is faith. He is the Living Word of God that we bear and who bears us. The armor of God is not something we wear like a coat or a pair of shoes. We "put it on" as we renew our minds to the Reality of our new life. The armor of God is the very character of Christ worked into our lives, beginning with our hearts, then our minds, then our entire being. The armor of God is His life in us.

That life covers, protects, equips, secures, positions, and empowers us for the call that has become our new life. Being a new creation in Christ empowers us for victory, for peace, and for a certain, purposeful future.

The armor of God, *Christness,* is the manifestation of the transforming power of the Cross. His resurrection life has now become ours as we yield ourselves to Him. The armor of God is invincible. In it, we can live with a heart that is open and tender, flexible and transparent, confident that Jesus will fight our battles and keep us through hard times. The armor of God makes us warriors of the King's army, competent to pursue and recover all.

Healing Prayer
for a Broken Heart

Lord, my heart has been wounded by words, actions, and thoughts that have stolen my peace and my faith.

The pain of these wounds has prompted me to shield my heart from receiving the love I crave and was created for.

I have not trusted You, and I'm sorry. Please forgive me for relying on my own ability to protect and direct my heart.

Pour in the water of your love to wash away the false armor of self-protection.

Pour in the oil of Your Spirit to soften the stony places that have festered into infections that threaten to destroy me.

Lay the ax to the root of every sinful response, every judgment, vow, or bitterroot that has supplanted the good ground of my heart.

Wash away every memory of pain and offense, and heal me with the healing blood of Jesus.

I forgive those who have hurt me and I release my judgments against them.

Reveal to me the lies I have believed that have kept me in bondage.

Help me to walk in the newness of a clean heart. I put on the whole armor of God as described in Ephesians 6.

I trust You to protect and keep me.

Thank you, Father, for your grace and love. I receive all the blessing You have for me. In Jesus' name. Amen.

RELATED SCRIPTURE (KJV)

1 Sam 17:47 And all this assembly shall know that the LORD saveth not with sword and spear: for the battle is the Lord's, and he will give you into our hands.

Rom 13:12 The night is far spent, the day is at hand: let us therefore cast off the works of darkness, and let us put on the armour of light.

Isa 11:5 And righteousness shall be the girdle of his loins, and faithfulness the girdle of his reins.

Gen 15:6 And he believed in the LORD; and he counted it to him for righteousness.

Job 29:14 I put on righteousness, and it clothed me: my judgment was as a robe and a diadem.

Rom 3:22 Even the righteousness of God which is by faith of Jesus Christ unto all and upon all them that believe: for there is no difference:

Rom 1:17 For therein is the righteousness of God revealed from faith to faith: as it is written, The just shall live by faith.

Heb 6:12 That ye be not slothful, but followers of them who through faith and patience inherit the promises.

Rom 14:17 For the kingdom of God is not meat and drink; but righteousness, and peace, and joy in the Holy Ghost.

Rom 5:18-19 Therefore as by the offence of one judgment came upon all men to condemnation; even so by the righteousness of one the free gift came upon all men unto justification of life. For as by one man's disobedience many were made sinners, so by the obedience of one shall many be made righteous.

1 Th 5:8-9 But let us, who are of the day, be sober, putting on the breastplate of faith and love; and for an helmet, the hope of salvation. For God hath not appointed us to wrath, but to obtain salvation by our Lord Jesus Christ.

John 14:6 Jesus saith unto him, I am the way, the truth, and the life: no man cometh unto the Father, but by me.

Mat 10:12-13 And when ye come into an house, salute it. And if the house be worthy, let your peace come upon it: but if it be not worthy, let your peace return to you.

Luke 1:78-79 Through the tender mercy of our God; whereby the dayspring from on high hath visited us, To give light to them that sit in darkness and in the shadow of death, to guide our feet into the way of peace.

Heb 4:12 For the word of God is quick, and powerful, and sharper than any two-edged sword, piercing even to the dividing asunder of soul and spirit, and of the joints and marrow, and is a discerner of the thoughts and intents of the heart.

John 15:3-4 Now ye are clean through the word which I have spoken unto you. Abide in me, and I in you. As the branch cannot bear fruit of itself, except it abide in the vine; no more can ye, except ye abide in me.

On the seventh day of Christness,
my Lord, He gave to me

SEVEN BLESSINGS FOR GIVING

1. **returns**

Give, and it shall be given unto you; good measure, pressed down, and shaken together, and running over, shall men give into your bosom. For with the same measure that ye mete withal it shall be measured to you again (Luke 6:38 KJV).

The point is this: the one who sows sparingly will also reap sparingly, and the one who sows bountifully will also reap bountifully (2 Cor. 9:6 NIV).

2. **reward**

And if anyone gives even a cup of cold water to one of these little ones because he is my disciple, I tell you the truth, he will certainly not lose his reward (Mat. 10:42 NIV).

3. **all grace abounding**

And God is able to make all grace abound to you, so that in all things at all times, having all that you need, you will abound in every good work (2 Cor. 9:8 NIV).

4. **<u>all sufficiency</u>**

And God is able to provide you with every blessing in abundance, so that by always having enough of everything, you may share abundantly in every good work (2 Cor. 9:8 NRSV).

5. **<u>eternal righteousness</u>**

As it is written, "He scatters abroad, he gives to the poor; his righteousness endures forever" (2 Cor. 9:9 NRSV).

6. **<u>increased fruits</u>**

He who supplies seed to the sower and bread for food will supply and multiply your seed for sowing and increase the harvest of your righteousness (2 Cor. 9:10 NRSV).

7. **<u>enrichment in all things</u>** [5]

You will be enriched in every way for your great generosity, which will produce thanksgiving to God through us (2 Cor. 9:11 NRSV).

Give…What image does this word put in your heart and your mind? Give. We hear it so often. *Give.*

I used to think I really understood what giving was all about. I spent my youth giving a lot. As a Girl Scout I gave my time and talents to supporting the vision and goals of our group. I gave my best efforts in school to get good grades. I gave my heart to those who said they loved me. I gave God my prayers. But all that giving was not of the God-kind. All that giving was really like "chumming the waters," putting in small fish so that bigger fish would come and take the bait. I was looking for love, for affirmation, for praise, for a sense of fulfillment, for an escape, for fun, and for attention. I was *giving to get.* Of course, I didn't realize it at the time.

I thought of myself as a giver, but I remember dishonoring my mother for all her giving. She gave her time, her talents, and her treasures to girls and other women in our community. I resented it; I felt like she had robbed *me*, and I attacked her verbally, wanting her to feel the hurt I did. I called her a "sucker" and a "fool." Years later, she stabbed me with my own words when I began to follow in her footsteps.

What caused me to become so bitter? I remember being jealous of others who had my mother's attention and who shared her joy. I didn't have that kind of relationship with my mother, and I wanted it. Seeing others getting what I believed should have been *mine* made me harden my heart against giving and against my mom. God had to heal my wounded heart so that I could receive the blessings of both her love and His good gifts.

It took many years to root out all that pain, but God did it, and even more. He gave me a love for my mom that I would have believed impossible in my past. God first healed me and then taught me to give her the God-kind-of-love that gives to free others from the demands and expectations of a needy heart. Trusting Him, I learned to keep my heart open to receive and, yes, even to be hurt again by careless words, knowing He would keep my heart.

It began with trusting God as my Parent, and allowing myself to seek my completeness, my protection, and my affirmation in Him. That opened the doors of my heart to receive even greater gifts from His heart that shame and lies had formerly kept me from embracing. I'm still a "work in progress," however. God still has areas of my heart that He is perfecting with His kind of love so I can live and love as He does.

We all have a wounded child still living in our hearts. We've all been hurt and disappointed, or even abused, by parents or others in authority in our young lives who, for whatever reason, could not give us all the unconditional love, the kind of attention and affirmation or the validation that we needed to thrive. Out of a needy heart we gave, like I did, to get what our hearts needed. But that need could never be fulfilled, that thirst could never be quenched because "stuff" could not replace the loving touch or the words that gave life.

When we were children some of us had trouble sharing or giving our "stuff" to others. Our little hearts were holding on to those things that made us feel loved, celebrated, or safe. We may have felt that giving would bring us lack or that we would be losing something that would leave a hole in our life. In our hearts there is still a little child that is protecting the heart that was robbed, wounded, and, for many, even broken.

So as adults when some of us hear the word "give," we restrain ourselves, allowing the spirit of bitterness and resentment to stop the free flow of love, of giving from our hearts. We cast aspersions and condemnation on those people and organizations who we feel are hankering for our dollar, our time, and our "stuff."

Why? Because our hearts have been repeatedly wounded. We felt manipulated by those we trusted, and our giving did not satisfy our heart's need. The world, as well as religion, entices us to give to get, promising prosperity as the reward. But that prosperity seems to elude many of us, and suspicion, and then, resentment supersede trust. The root of the problem lies in the motivation, just as it did to the child's heart that gave to get its needs fulfilled— giving with "strings attached" we sometimes call it.

It's not until we have received His heart in the "great exchange" that we can truly give with the agape love that now keeps us. But even after we are born again, we often struggle with giving. We struggle because we still think we have to *do* something to get what we need, even from God. We struggle because our minds have not been renewed or *Christed* in the area of giving. The *Christed* mind and heart gives as God directs, with no legalistic limitations or mandates; it gives as an imminent act of praise and obedience in trust.

Some argue that tithing, for example, is a legalistic act; others argue that tithing is one of the universal laws of God. The issue is settled if we are giving from our heart. Giving is an act of the heart. The hardened heart believes that God is not perfectly committed to our well-being. It still believes lies, serving a "Santa Claus God."

Men hoard; Satan steals; God gives.

Giving is the very heart of God. God gave His own life in His Son because He would rather die than live without us. God gave good gifts and even gave His own life to us *now* in the presence and the power of the Holy Spirit so that we might be blessed with an abundant life *now*.

God does not hoard. In Him is no lack, no need, no insecurity, no fear, no want, no hardship. In Him is only fullness to overflowing. He is the giver of a life that far exceeds anything we can even dream up, and He has given all of that life to us in Christ. He is not holding back any good thing from us.

For the believer experiencing any form of lack, security can be found in the arms of the Father who waits to bless His child with a "robe, a ring, and a fatted calf" (cf. parable of the prodigal son). The Bible says that God rains on both the sinner and the saint, the just and the unjust. That means that His blessings are for all who walk in accordance with His universal laws.

One of those universal laws is the law of giving. In the Kingdom of God, one *increases* by decreasing, *multiplies* by dividing, *receives* by giving, *lives* by dying, becomes *first* by being last. The Kingdom of God holds nothing back—not treasure, not love, not forgiveness, not talents, not any good thing.

The law of giving is simple. Give and it shall be given unto you, "pressed down shaken together, and running over," (Luke 6:38) with returns "some 30, some 60, some 100 fold" (Mark 4:8). The law of giving is one of God's universal laws. It reflects His nature and His purpose.

We see this law working in the business world. One does not have to be saved in order to reap blessings from God. He or she has only to follow the universal laws of God. One look at entrepreneurs like the Rockefellers, or more recently, Sam Walton and Bill Gates, can attest to the validity and the surety of the law of giving.

Their giving has only resulted in greater and greater assets with increase in their own personal finances. This is the law of God in action. And it is just as true for you and for me as it was and is for anyone who gives with a willing and cheerful heart.

Men hoard. Satan steals. God gives.

Let's get this one thing settled. God is not holding back any good thing from His children (Ps 84:11), and we are His children (1Jn 3:2). We are living according to the laws of God whether we believe it or not. God's love for us is the giving kind, and the Bible says He gives only good gifts to his children. Bad things do not come from God. There is no evil in Him. Bad things are the consequences or fruit of the universal laws of God in action. That's why we need to know them. Universal laws are absolute.

Another expression of the law of giving is the law of sowing and reaping. But with God involved, that law has a bonus—increase. When God established the laws of the universe, it was for our gain.

So, being the very big God that He is, and loving us with more love than we can imagine, He added the law of increase to the law of sowing and reaping. One has only to look at an ear of corn, or a simple fruit tree to see that this law is utterly true. In the world, we have expressions like "things happen in 3's," "what goes around comes around," and "when it rains, it pours." That's the law of sowing and reaping with increase, also known as the law of giving.

Satan steals (John 10:10). Don't you know that there is a contract out on your life and the treasures of your heart? We have so many questions during bad times. "Where was God?" "If God is so good, then why do bad things happen to good people?"

God, our Father, never leaves or forsakes us. But we must consider that His Kingdom is not the "way of the world." His Kingdom and ours are established by universal laws. Those laws are established in and out of time, and He cannot and will not change them.

They create the very fiber of the universe. They are our anchor and our hope, our comfort and our peace. Knowing them, we can trust God because He does not change; knowing them we can run to Him, because His love for us is unconditional.

The thief isn't God. The thief is the one who whispered lies into your heart that you have always believed about yourself and others, including God, your Father. The thief is the one who made you feel ashamed and unworthy, made you feel that you needed to hide from God and others. The thief is the one who told you that you couldn't trust God, and that you had to take care of yourself. The thief is the one who told you that you had to "earn" all the blessings that God says are yours by faith. The thief is the one who spoke fear, mistrust, shame, unbelief, and lack into your heart. Whose report will you believe?

What kingdom do you want to live in? Jesus told the disciples to tell the people that the Kingdom of God has come to this earth—*now!* (Luke 10:9) And so now, that is *now*, we have a choice. The kingdom of man, of time and circumstances, of self-will, of self-love, of hoarding is under the lease of the thief. But Jesus said that His kingdom has come. In Christ we can live in this kingdom—now—and we can sow and reap with increase the blessings of a God who would rather die than live without us.

In whichever kingdom we choose to live, we will live by the universal laws of God. Giving, sowing and reaping with increase, is one of those pivotal laws. As we live in the Kingdom of God, our circumstances in the kingdom of man will not rule our hearts and our minds. Giving God our trust and obedience in every situation, we can abide in the rest that keeps our hearts in peace. Our circumstances *will* change. Or we may choose to abide in the kingdom of man—subject to the circumstances and self-preservation that keep us stuck and struggling to gain or keep what we "have."

Give.... Are we beginning to see another picture? Are we beginning to see that God is *willing* to give us whatever we require to become healed, secure, and lacking in no good thing? Are we also beginning to see that we have choices? Our Father wants us to be free—free to choose, free to love, free to receive and free to give. "It was for freedom that Christ set us free" (Gal. 5:1).

There is no condemnation for anyone in Christ (Rom. 8:1). We are free to give...or not. What stops us is our heart, the fainting heart that needs healing and a touch of God. Do you find yourself hoarding? Mistrusting? Resenting? Maybe you need a heart transplant, or perhaps, only a "remodeling" job by the Builder and the Furnisher (Heb. 3:4). A healed heart is a giving heart. A loved heart is a loving heart. A *Christed* heart is a generous heart.

Now we have more opportunities to give than we think, for money is not the only asset that we possess to be a blessing to God and to others. The Scripture makes this clear. We have been given talents and well as treasure, time as well as tender. And we are called to give these gifts as well.

Putting first things first, we give God, our Father, our Savior, our Lord, thanks and honor. We do this in song, in prayer, in praise and in worship. We give thanks.

We don't all do that the same way and there is no formula, except, perhaps, "by the heart." Some dance and sing; some shout and laugh; some weep and sigh. Some praise with instruments; some praise with words and some with whispers. First, we give God honor, praise, and worship for He is worthy.

Acknowledging His great salvation and His love and provision for us, we glorify Him by our trust and complete reliance in His direction and call for our lives. We glorify Him by our dependence upon Him for our every need. This giving blesses God.

Praise opens the doors of heaven and ushers us into the presence of God. In that glory God provides every need. How do we get what we need from the realm of the glory to our realm of time? We bring it in by the power of our words spoken in faith. Declare and decree those things to be in faith, knowing that you are speaking God's will.

How do we know it is God's will? First, we know because it has already been spoken in His Word; next, we know by the peace of our own hearts. We know by the witness of others whom we trust for wise counsel. Finally, we know because there is no doubt or swerving in our own hearts. We continue to press in for the goal by standing on that Word, letting patience complete its perfect work with faith.

We give God our praise, our thanks, and our faith from our heart. He gives us His life, His promise, and His security that He not only hears but also answers our prayers and requests.

The Bible says that "the earth shall be filled with the knowledge of the glory of the Lord, as the waters cover the sea" (Hab. 2:14). The Bible says we go from "glory to glory," from one open door to the next. Losing sight of ourselves, we become more Christ-minded than earthly minded. That translates us from the realm of fear to faith, from lack to luxury, from weakness to wholeness.

Praise fills our hearts with faith and strength. Out of that overflow we can give others encouragement, exhortation, and enthusiasm for the things of God. We give others the plate of blessings that we have tasted, neither force-feeding nor brow-beating them with the gift! We are serving a love feast! And it's meant to bless, strengthen, and woo us to receive more of God.

We give time, first to God, then to others. First, to God, we give time to praise, worship, reading, exhortation, and doctrine (1 Tim. 4:13). Time in the Word is a love feast, and it transforms our minds as an overflow of a touched heart. Through it we come to know our standing in Christ, our inheritance as sons and daughters, our call of destiny. Through giving time to the Word we are empowered, transformed, and translated into kingdom living *here and now.* We give God praise and thanksgiving, and we give God time studying His Word, the Scriptures.

But there is even more that we can give. We also know that we have been given gifts, both natural and supernatural, that profit ourselves and others. The Bible tells us to give ourselves wholly to the gifts that are within us, and our profiting will appear to all (1 Tim. 4:14-15).

We usually recognize our giftings as the best part of ourselves, the part of our makeup that we didn't earn or acquire by any activities of our own. Our gifts may be talents or character traits or supernatural abilities given to us by God. Our talents are not only for our enjoyment, but also for the blessing to others.

We give ourselves to our giftings because they must be matured by practice of use, often developed by instruction, submitting to others with similar giftings. We go to school or take lessons to develop our gifts. We practice them while we are learning. We learn from correction as well as instruction. The list is infinite. Those gifts include character traits such as hospitality, wisdom, and encouragement in addition to the abilities we develop for personal or professional growth.

As an adult, I recognize giftings and talents that God has birthed and developed in me. Some of them are compassion, encouragement, leadership, and teaching. What giftings do you recognize in your own life? God has given us all wonderful gifts that He wants us to give ourselves "wholly" toward. That means He wants us to develop and perfect them by use of practice, not just for our own benefit and enjoyment, but also for His pleasure and for others' profit. There are other kinds of giftings, too, that God has given us.

The Bible tells us about supernatural giftings, or manifestations of the Holy Spirit that God gives when we are born again. One may have a call to heal the sick, preach the Gospel, or bind up the broken hearted. Paul talks about the nine "gifts" or "manifestations" of the Spirit in Galatians 5. (There's a whole chapter about them in "Day 9" of this book.) These supernatural gifts are God's character in us to love and minister to our own hearts and then to others. They are supernatural because they are birthed in the Spirit, in the Kingdom of God. They are the power of God to overcome whatever the enemy sends to discourage, rob, and destroy us. Like natural giftings, these, too, need to be nurtured and perfected by practice and submission to the Spirit of God.

The Bible says that the giftings of God are irrevocable

(Rom. 11:29). God will not call them back, or take them away from you once He has given them. Gifts are not the result of achievements or good works on our part. They are free and He will not take them back! He gives us good gifts so that we can have a good life (John 10:10).

God tells us in the book of Jeremiah that He has a plan for our lives, to give us a hope and a future. When we move in the destiny and plan that God has for us, not only do we benefit wholly, but so do others. We do that, in part, by giving ourselves to the gifts that are within us.

Now we have seen that our first fruits of giving are thanks and praise to God; then we give time to studying His Word, the Bible. Next, we give ourselves wholly to the giftings He has deposited into us, developing them and then using them to bless Him, ourselves, and others. There is still something else the Bible says we can give.

The Bible calls us to give "holy things." [6] These gifts are the touch of God that we cannot explain away, that we recognize are supernatural. These are the gifts which beckon others to follow Christ, and to receive His love and His life into their own. They are the same works that Jesus did in His earthly ministry. They are the "holy things."

When we walk in the revelation of our *Christed* identity, the "new man," we will also do the works of Jesus Christ, giving His life to others as the outpouring of His love. "Every good and perfect gift is from above, coming down from the Father of the heavenly lights, who does not change like shifting shadows" (James 1:17 NIV) .

The gifts He has given us so freely have profited us and others spiritually, emotionally, and often, financially. Our thanks, our time, our talents, our treasures and our love are all we have to give—first to God and then to others. Giving is an act of the heart. It is the response of being *Christed*, of being blessed not by our earnings but by God's generous personal love.

Giving is the best response we have to receiving. Giving from the heart, freely, with no "strings attached," is the agape life of Christ living itself through us to others.

God does not give to get. He gives because it is His very nature. The only thing that God is giving Himself is an everlasting Name. And even that blesses and benefits us. He has given us the legal authority of the Name of Jesus Christ to do the works of Christ on earth. It is by the power of His Name that we bring the Kingdom of God to the kingdom of man.

Let us give, and give, and give. God *gives.* We are literally His children in Christ. And we are so much like our Daddy, that we *give—just like Him!*

Just like my Daddy

When folks look at me they often say
I look a lot like my daddy.
That makes me happy because
My dad is my best friend.
It wasn't always that way.
No, there was a lot of strife and hurt
That caused deep, deep chasms
That separated us from the love that
God had always intended.

But when I learned and then practiced
the power of forgiveness
Things between us began to change.
It wasn't easy at first.
I learned to accept him
Just the way he was.
I learned to receive what he had to give.
I learned to enjoy the good and let go of the bad.
I let my dad know I needed him
to be my cheerleader and my friend.
I let him know he was valuable to me
Just the way he was.

The best years were the last years
we shared and spent together.
We laughed a lot and we wept, too,
knowing that time was running short.
Now when I'm called my father's daughter
I celebrate and stand a little taller.
My dad opened my heart to receive
Both his and our Father's blessing that will
always keep me in the giving zone.
I want to be just like my Daddy.

RELATED SCRIPTURES (KJV)

Mat 7:9-10 Or what man is there of you, whom if his son ask bread, will he give him a stone? Or if he ask a fish, will he give him a serpent?

Mat 10:8 Heal the sick, cleanse the lepers, raise the dead, cast out devils: freely ye have received, freely give.

Mat 11:28 Come unto me, all ye that labour and are heavy laden, and I will give you rest.

Mat 16:19 And I will give unto thee the keys of the kingdom of heaven:

Mat 20:28 Even as the Son of man came not to be ministered unto, but to minister, and to give his life a ransom for many.

Luke 6:38 Give, and it shall be given unto you; good measure, pressed down, and shaken together, and running over, shall men give into your bosom. For with the same measure that ye mete withal it shall be measured to you again.

Luke 10:19 Behold, I give unto you power to tread on serpents and scorpions, and over all the power of the enemy: and nothing shall by any means hurt you.

Luke 11:3 Give us day by day our daily bread.

Luke 12:33-34 Sell that ye have, and give alms; provide yourselves bags which wax not old, a treasure in the heavens that faileth not, where no thief approacheth, neither moth corrupteth. For where your treasure is, there will your heart be also.

John 4:14 But whosoever drinketh of the water that I shall give him shall never thirst; but the water that I shall give him shall be in him a well of water springing up into everlasting life.

Acts 6:4 But we will give ourselves continually to prayer, and to the ministry of the word.

2 Cor 9:7-8 Every man according as he purposeth in his heart, so let him give; not grudgingly, or of necessity: for God loveth a cheerful giver. And God is able to make all grace abound toward you; that ye, always having all sufficiency in all things, may abound to every good work:

Eph 4:27 Neither give place to the devil.

1 Th 5:18 In every thing give thanks: for this is the will of God in Christ Jesus concerning you.

1 Tim 4:13.15 Till I come, give attendance to reading, to exhortation, to doctrine. Meditate upon these things; give thyself wholly to them; that thy profiting may appear to all.

Rev 2:6-7 And he said unto me, It is done. I am Alpha and Omega, the beginning and the end. I will give unto him that is athirst of the fountain of the water of life freely. He that hath an ear, let him hear what the Spirit saith unto the churches; To him that overcometh will I give to eat of the tree of life, which is in the midst of the paradise of God.

Rev 2:26 And he that overcometh, and keepeth my works unto the end, to him will I give power over the nations:

On the eighth day of Christness
my Lord, He gave to me

EIGHT 'TUDES WITH PROMISE

MATTHEW 5:3-12 (KJV)

Blessed are the poor in spirit: for theirs is the kingdom of heaven.

Blessed are they that mourn: for they shall be comforted.

Blessed are the meek: for they shall inherit the earth.

Blessed are they which do hunger and thirst after righteousness: for they shall be filled.

Blessed are the merciful: for they shall obtain mercy.

Blessed are the pure in heart: for they shall see God.

Blessed are the peacemakers: for they shall be called the children of God.

Blessed are they which are persecuted for righteousness' sake: for theirs is the kingdom of heaven.

Blessed are ye, when men shall revile you, and persecute you, and shall say all manner of evil against you falsely, for my sake.

Rejoice, and be exceeding glad: for great is your reward in heaven: for so persecuted they the prophets which were before you.

BLESSED

happy,

enviably fortunate,

and spiritually prosperous,

possessing the happiness

produced by the experience of God's favor

and especially conditioned by

the revelation of His grace,

regardless of their outward

conditions,

with life-joy

and satisfaction

in God's favor and salvation.

(Matt. 5:3 Amplified version of "blessed")

The amplification of "blessed" fills me with wonder and even awe. Being "enviably fortunate and spiritually prosperous" is a position of great wealth and power. Prosperity gives power to its possessor. The world knows that; it has made financial prosperity one of its idols. But this spiritual wealth is of an even higher realm. It is the wealth, the prosperity, of the Spirit.

We know that the wealth of the world buys riches, power and position. And we also know that this is a temporary advantage. This is wealth that can be lost, stolen, or simply depleted. We know that this wealth belongs to a realm that is itself temporal. This realm will pass away, and so will everything in it. We also know that we will also pass away, and that we can't take our worldly wealth with us.

But these verses are talking about an altogether different kind of prosperity, a different kind of power and wealth that touches every form of prosperity in every realm. It is birthed in the realm of the spirit and lives in the realm of the spirit. This is the realm that is not bound to the realm of time, but it manifests in time.

This realm has kingdoms with inhabitants, a King, power and riches, and even wars. This is the realm inhabited by God and His angels. In this realm God rules by His Word. In this realm we even co-reign with Him as we declare and decree His Word with our own mouths. The realm of the spirit influences the realm of the natural, carnal man, and the realms of time, space, and the senses. The Kingdom of God manifests in our own realm of time and space, too. It is the kingdom to which we are called. It is the kingdom for which we were created.

The Kingdom of God is the realm of the glory, of the miraculous, of the "zoe" life of God which supersedes, or overrides, the realm of the natural world. This is the creative realm of the living Word, which, when spoken in the God-kind-of-faith, manifests that which it proclaims, the same realm revealed in Genesis 1 at creation.

This is the realm of the New Creation Person, who has been born again of the Spirit of God, whose position is sure and whose inheritance is all the promises of God given in His Word. This is the realm of prosperity that is not bound to time, to decay, or to change. It is an enviable position, but to everyone who would call upon the Name of the Lord in faith, it is available.

This is the prosperity that possesses "the happiness produced by the experience of God's favor and especially conditioned by the revelation of His grace, regardless of their outward conditions, with life-joy and satisfaction in God's favor and salvation" (Matt. 5:3 AMP). Let us break this down into bites that we can savor.

To be blessed is to have the favor of God. That means He is aware of our circumstances, our needs, our hopes and our desires. That means that He has purposed to give us good things. What does that include? Think about it. What would you ask from God? What do you need? That is only just the beginning of the blessings that God, our Father, desires to give you.

The Bible says that it hasn't even occurred to us, that we

can't even begin to envision the blessings that He has for those who love Him. "But as it is written, Eye hath not seen, nor ear heard, neither have entered into the heart of man, the things which God hath prepared for them that love him" (1 Cor. 2:9).

How can we begin to receive such an abundant life? How can we actually walk in these blessings that will make us whole, that will be "more than enough" to meet our circumstances, our heart's needs, and the compassion that pours out of our hearts toward others? We can begin to become aware of grace as a dynamic of our lives, *here and now*.

Grace is often described as God's unmerited favor upon our lives, or God's redemption at Christ's expense. Grace is the power of God to accomplish what we cannot do on our own; it is the power to walk into that new vision without effort. It is the power to forgive that unforgivable offense that wrenched our heart. It is the power to rest in times of turmoil and upheaval. It is the overwhelming love of God touching our lives at the point of our need. We can't earn it because it is a gift, freely given, that empowers us to live the Christed life.

God gives it to us at our conception, and woos us with it to the point of a personal encounter with Him that brings us into a new birth of our spirit. Grace then keeps us in the abiding place with Him, and favors us with mercy, abundance, and love. Grace is the free gift of salvation. It pours from the cross of Calvary.

Salvation comes from the Greek word, "sodzo." Strong's Concordance defines it as "safe; to save, i.e. deliver or protect (lit. or fig.):--heal, preserve, save (self), do well, be (make) whole." (G4982) This salvation is an experience of complete and utter wholeness. In it there is no suffering, no lack or sickness. Incidentally, it is also the meaning of the Hebrew word, "shalom." Peace and joy are an outward testimony that our salvation is at work in our lives regardless of the circumstances that may speak otherwise.

It doesn't mean that we are free of the trials and sorrows of life, but that we have the grace, the power in Christ, not to be tossed to and fro like a wave in a tempest. God's grace will show us how to be freed from the consequences that may be the fruits of our earlier judgments. Grace will free us from the generational or word curses that infect our hearts. Grace will show the path from the lies and the shame that keeps us hiding from the One who loves us most. The salvation (sodzo) of God in Christ heals our brokenness, transforms our mind, and empowers our spirit to live wholeheartedly. Our times are ordered; our paths are secure; our relationships are growing.

Finally, we are "satisfied." We are not distressed when calamity strikes. We are, as Paul says, not ruled by our natural circumstances. Dependent upon our Father, relying on His Word and His promises, we now speak to our situations according to the Word of God. We speak with the faith established in our heart that He knows our situations and will be faithful to fulfill His promise in our lives. And we rest with confidence in God.

I have a friend who lives this "sodzo" life of God. I have never heard her complain or feel sorry for herself, though she and her family have experienced their share of struggle and distress. She is one who looks at Jesus at the cross, and says that if God never gave her another thing, that His sacrifice at the cross was more than she ever deserved. She walks in an attitude of gratitude for all things, and takes the great commission to heart, "minding other people's business" and bringing them to Jesus. God has never left her, forsaken her, or dishonored her faith. On the contrary, she is highly favored, enviably fortunate, and spiritually prosperous. Her children call her blessed. Her satisfaction is in Christ, and not reliant on her condition. To the world she is an anathema. But to the spirit realm, she is the child of God, walking in the promise and the prosperity of her position in Christ. Her life reminds me that the way up is down, that promotion comes from reliance upon God, that peace and prosperity are not measured by money or worldly possessions.

That is the message of the Scripture we call the "Sermon on the Mount" containing these eight "beatitudes." The blessing comes to the person who seeks God, who depends upon Him, who constantly stays hungry and thirsty for the things of God in the realm of the Spirit.

Staying hungry is our part. How do we stay in that place of blessing? The answer is simpler than we can imagine. Hunger comes from developing a taste for the glory of God. Having come to that banqueting table, that intimate place with God where we drink from His Spirit, we can now be satisfied with no less.

How do we get to that table? We get there by one–on-One fellowship, through worship, through prayer, through living in the Word, by the power of the Spirit. We get there by asking with a humble heart, desperate for Him, seeking His presence more than His presents. The blessing comes to the one who stays separated from the lusts or pollutions of the world, who gives up the right to be right in order to promote peace and reconciliation. The blessing comes when we yield to His life in us.

The Beatitudes are the blessings that Jesus described in His sermon on the mount. They are seeming paradoxes, showing that the Kingdom of God is totally different from the kingdom of the natural man. The Beatitudes are promises, and we can go even farther and say that they are the constitution for the Kingdom of God on this earth.

The promises of blessings are for those who mourn, are poor in spirit, and are meek, merciful, and pure in heart. They are for those who stay hungry and thirsty for righteousness, and for those who make peace. The promises of blessing are for the persecuted and for the reviled, for those who will not walk in the way of the world's corrupt paradigms of success.

That should comfort most of us. Life isn't a "bowl of cherries," unless you include the pits. The fragrance and beauty of a rose is also accompanied by thorns. Many folks are afraid to confess that they are being blessed; they think that their confession will bring about calamity. That is a lot of superstitious hogwash!

God in His Word tells us that life is full of trials and tribulations. And He adds in the next breath not to grieve, for He has overcome the world. "These things I have spoken unto you, that in me ye might have peace. In the world ye shall have tribulation: but be of good cheer; I have overcome the world" (John 16:33).

The Beatitudes give us a picture of God's hand in our

persecuted, sorrowful, hard times. "Blessed are they that mourn, for they shall be comforted." He tells us that He is here, in the midst of our trials. He gives us His shoulder to lean on, His heart to drink from, His strength to walk in, and His ability to move in. The person who is in the midst of the battle can take strength and comfort from these words. The temptation in those times is to be overwhelmed by the circumstances that invade our days, and even our nights, as our peace and faith are attacked, as discouragement and fear try to create a stronghold in our hearts. The Beatitudes remind us that the Kingdom of God is truly "at hand." The battles that are coming against us are the enemy's attempt to remove us from the Kingdom that is being established in our hearts and lives. Truly, the battle is the Lord's, but we are still in His army, and we cannot leave our posts.

Jesus is our role model. His earthly ministry was a picture of the power and the breadth of the Beatitudes. This is the picture of the Messiah who leads by example, walking in the power of the Spirit rather than in His own natural strength. Jesus is the picture of the overcoming life. Though "in" the world, He was not "of" it. He lived by the rules and the by-laws of the Kingdom of God expressed in the Beatitudes. Persecution and sorrow came, but they never had a stronghold in His heart.

This is the picture of the separated life that hungers and thirsts for the life of the spirit, denying the flesh its carnal desires and leanings. Jesus was tempted just as we are. He came to the Father often seeking comfort, strength, and direction.

We don't know about many of these encounters, but we have the witness of one of them. In the garden of Gethsemane

Jesus prayed to His Father that the cup would be removed from Him. He sought to forego the agony of the cross, just as any man would. But His Father said no.

"Blessed are they which are persecuted for righteousness' sake: for theirs is the kingdom of heaven. Blessed are ye, when men shall revile you, and persecute you, and shall say all manner of evil against you falsely, for my sake." I believe that the Father said more than "no," but I do know that Jesus chose to obey and honor His Father, and endure the cross for our sakes. Walking in the laws of heaven, He was reviled and persecuted for not compromising the favor of God for the favor of man, for not fearing and yielding to the pressure of peers or religion or the status quo. Jesus lived in the Kingdom of God by the power of the Holy Spirit, and so can we.

The Beatitudes show us the source of our power and might. They reveal the very presence of God as He is moving in our lives. We can live in His presence *now*. We *must* find a way to get there when the battle rages. For there our victory lies. This is the table He has prepared for us in the presence of our enemies (Ps. 23:5).

The Beatitudes give us a picture of God's agape love, the "love feast" that nurtures, fills, and strengthens us for the new day. In them we see God giving mercy and favor to the needy, bringing good news of deliverance and healing to the hurting.

This is a picture of the way to victory, empowerment, and great reward. This is *not* the picture of the world's definition of becoming successful, powerful, or happy. For God, the way up is down.

What are the promises? They are too many to tell. The Beatitudes are simply a broad summary of the rewards of the *Christed* life. "Blessed are the poor in spirit: for theirs is the kingdom of heaven." The kingdom of heaven is the realm of the Spirit of God, the realm of His glory, His presence, and His favor and grace. Jesus told us that the kingdom of God has come to earth. Abiding in the kingdom of heaven gives us not only a whole new perspective of our circumstances and times, it actually gives us dominion over them. We stay there by practice!

"Blessed are they which do hunger and thirst after righteousness: for they shall be filled." Walking in righteousness, we have intimate fellowship with our Father through Christ. Like Abraham, we walk with our Father as if sin has never touched us, for we have been washed pure by the blood of the Lamb. The righteousness that covers us is like the robe that the father put on his prodigal son. It restored him to the family, declared not only his kinship, but also his authority in that house. That robe honored him as a treasured son.

The righteousness that covers us in Christ does no less. It restores us to God's family in right relationship. It declares not only our kinship, but also our authority. His robe of righteousness honors us as a treasured son and daughter. Once again, we can know intimacy with our Father.

"Blessed are the meek: for they shall inherit the earth." The world thinks of meekness as weakness. But the kingdom of God calls it strength, and even power. It means that we recognize that in our own strength we can do nothing. Meekness is a sign of reliance on God from the heart. Meekness utterly trusts a personal God who loves us.

Meekness allows the power of God to flow through us. Knowing the Father's heart, following Him just as Jesus did, we may ask whatever we will, and, by the power and authority of the Name of Jesus, we may proclaim the kingdom of heaven's blessings upon this earth just as Jesus did. That is how we inherit the earth.

We are called to reclaim the land. We were given authority over all things of the earth in Adam. The earth is the Lord's and the fullness thereof (Ps. 24:1). And it is ours; it is part of our inheritance (Gen. 1:28-30, Matt. 18:18). Meekness will restore to us the blessing of possessing the earth that we lost in Eden.

"Blessed are the peacemakers: for they shall be called the children of God." Now walking in righteousness, we *are* the children of God, sharing, His divine nature through Jesus Christ. We are not swayed to and fro by the wiles of evil in our midst. Now we are led by the inner peace that abides in our hearts and minds.

This is the peace Jesus says He gives us (Jn 14:27). It is not of this world or kingdom; it is of His kingdom. So this world cannot take it away. This is the peace that gave Jesus rest when all His disciples were terrorized by a storm that threatened to break up their boat. This is the peace that let Jesus stay behind to minister for three days after Lazarus had died, or had "fallen asleep" as Jesus put it. He knew that Lazarus would rise when He called him forth from the tomb. He did not have to rush to the scene when the crisis came. He walked there in peace. This is the peace that carried Jesus through Gethsemane. It is the same peace that kept Jesus through Calvary and even through Hell before His resurrection. This is the same peace that He leaves us.

The book of Jeremiah (Jer. 1:8-12 KJV) gives us a beautiful picture of the *Christed* life in action.

> Be not afraid of their faces: for I am with thee to deliver thee, saith the LORD. Then the LORD put forth his hand, and touched my mouth. And the LORD said unto me, Behold, I have put my words in thy mouth. See, I have this day set thee over the nations and over the kingdoms, to root out, and to pull down, and to destroy, and to throw down, to build, and to plant. Moreover the word of the LORD came unto me, saying, Jeremiah, what seest thou? And I said, I see a rod of an almond tree. Then said the LORD unto me, Thou hast well seen: for I will hasten my word to perform it.

Jesus moved upon the earth in righteousness, mercy, and power, revealing the love of God with mercy, purity, peace, and compassion. We are called to do the same as keepers of the Kingdom.

We have the promise of protection and of deliverance from all evil that comes against us. By our standing in the kingdom of heaven, we live a life yielded to the will of God. His Words are in our mouth and we can have what we speak through faith in Him who said them first (Mark 11: 24).

Jesus came to the earth to root out evil from our hearts

and to pull down the powers and principalities that ruled in high places. He came to throw down the all the plots of the enemy, and to build the kingdom of God. He came to plant the tree of life and righteousness in our hearts by paying the price for sin. He lived the perfect life and then by His own meekness, laid it down. His public ministry modeled the kingdom come to earth in a human heart. Through the power of resurrection, it's now ours.

The Sermon on the Mount reminds us that the ways of God are not the ways of the world. There He showed us eight attitudes, or lifestyle characteristics, that characterize the believer. By walking in the Spirit of God we shall bear the fruits of the realm of His kingdom on earth. We are promised victory, joy, peace, and the very presence of God in our lives. Not as the world gives, God's rewards are sure and eternal. We are *blessed.*

RELATED SCRIPTURES (KJV)

1 Pet 3:3-4   Whose adorning let it not be that outward adorning of plaiting the hair, and of wearing of gold, or of putting on of apparel; But let it be the hidden man of the heart, in that which is not corruptible, even the ornament of a meek and quiet spirit, which is in the sight of God of great price.

Mark 10:14 But when Jesus saw it, he was much displeased, and said unto them, Suffer the little children to come unto me, and forbid them not: for of such is the kingdom of God.

Luke 22:29 And I appoint unto you a kingdom, as my Father hath appointed unto me;

Isa 61:3   To appoint unto them that mourn in Zion, to give unto them beauty for ashes, the oil of joy for mourning, the garment of praise for the spirit of heaviness; that they might be called trees of righteousness, the planting of the LORD, that he might be glorified.

Isa 55:1-2   Ho, every one that thirsteth, come ye to the waters, and he that hath no money; come ye, buy, and eat; yea, come, buy wine and milk without money and without price. Wherefore do ye spend money for that which is not bread? and your labour for that which satisfieth not? hearken diligently unto me, and eat ye that which is good, and let your soul delight itself in fatness.

Rom 5:18 Therefore as by the offence of one judgment came upon all men to condemnation; even so by the righteousness of one the free gift came upon all men unto justification of life.

Rom 9:30   What shall we say then? That the Gentiles, which followed not after righteousness, have attained to righteousness, even the righteousness which is of faith.

Heb 12:14 Follow peace with all men, and holiness, without which no man shall see the Lord:

1 John 3:2 Beloved, now are we the sons of God, and it doth not yet appear what we shall be: but we know that, when he shall appear, we shall be like him; for we shall see him as he is.

Rom 8:14 For as many as are led by the Spirit of God, they are the sons of God.

1 Pet 3:14 But and if ye suffer for righteousness' sake, happy are ye: and be not afraid of their terror, neither be troubled;

James 3:17-18 But the wisdom that is from above is first pure, then peaceable, gentle, and easy to be entreated, full of mercy and good fruits, without partiality, and without hypocrisy. And the fruit of righteousness is sown in peace of them that make peace.

James 4:10 Humble yourselves in the sight of the Lord, and he shall lift you up.

2 Cor 4:9 Persecuted, but not forsaken; cast down, but not destroyed;

Titus 3:5 Not by works of righteousness which we have done, but according to his mercy he saved us, by the washing of regeneration, and renewing of the Holy Ghost;

John 15:16 Ye have not chosen me, but I have chosen you, and ordained you, that ye should go and bring forth fruit, and that your fruit should remain: that whatsoever ye shall ask of the Father in my name, he may give it you.

**On the ninth day of Christness,
my Lord, He gave to me**

NINE FRUITS OF THE SPIRIT

GALATIANS 5: 22-23 (KJV)
But the fruit of the Spirit is love, joy, peace,
longsuffering, gentleness, goodness, faith, meekness,
temperance: against such there is no law.

The Fruits of the Spirit

*We do not need to struggle to achieve them,
and we do not need to pray to receive them.*

*We HAVE them when the Holy Spirit
makes His abode in our hearts!*

*They are the fruits of the
        yielded and transformed life,*

 *the gifts that make us
        the fruitbearers on the vine:
            revealing agape love,
    the God-kind-of-love
        to a lost and hungry world;*

JOY, unspeakable and full of glory;
        gladness not dependent upon circumstances,
        our source of strength;

PEACE that leads and guides the paths of our lives,
        heart-rest;

LONGSUFFERING,
        patience with unconditional love
        and forbearance;

FAITH , the substance of things hoped for,
        the assurance of the outcome
            that gives us the boldness to act;

GENTLENESS, the kind of goodness that
        makes us feel loved
            even when we do wrong;

GOODNESS, OR BENEVOLENCE,
        the gift of the cheerful giver;

HUMILITY, not self-abasement,
        but self-acceptance
            in the light of the finished work of Christ
                on our behalf;

SELF CONTROL, renewing our mind
            by the washing of the Word of God,
        and going forth
            in authority and power
        in the God-kind-of-love,
            living in the Spirit,
        in the nature and life of our Father.

It all began for us in a garden. God created the universe and everything in it. Then He created a garden for His most precious creation, the one made in His image and likeness—man and woman. The heavens were already prepared to be lights and signs to His new creation. The angels were already created to serve God and His new creation, to bring messages and to protect God's most precious child. The seas and the mountains, the plants with their seed, the fish and the birds, and the animals great and small had been prepared to bless the child and the seed of the King. One third of this assembly of the heavenly host had already fallen away from the Truth, and was cast out of heaven. Then God planted a garden.

The triune God created Adam in His own image and likeness. Out of Adam's side, God brought forth Eve, who shared Adam's nature and essence. She was created to be his mate who would provide the God-kind of help. Hers was a position of esteem and honor. Their nature was God's nature, sharing qualities and characteristics of their Father as His children.

It is important to meditate on this vital truth because out of it comes understanding of the finished work of Christ on our behalf. How fantastic to believe that we are so like our Father! His very nature is our nature.

We have no problem identifying with the attributes and characteristics of our earthly parents. We recognize physical as well as emotional inheritances; we even look to generational history to recognize inherent talents and abilities. How then do we fail to recognize our own identification with the God who created us in His own image and likeness?

Man was created by God from the dust of the earth so that man would share in the essence of the earth and also identify with it. And he was given the breath of life by the Spirit of God, which is the essence and nature of the eternal God, so that man would share and identify with that, too. The soulish realm—the mind, will and emotional character of man—was polluted and turned self-ward after the fall. We were created in Adam in the God-state to walk with Him and to talk with Him.

Before God created Adam, He prepared a place for him. It was a garden. A garden is a protected and cultivated place. The Hebrew root of this word means to hedge about, protect, and defend. The garden prepared for the new creation was under a covenant of protection. God gave dominion, absolute authority and headship over it and the rest of the earth to His children, Adam and Eve. He put angels at the gates to defend the garden and its inhabitants from attack.

He commanded Adam and Eve to be fruitful and multiply, to fill the earth, and to subdue it using all its vast resources in the service of God and man. He gave them dominion over the fish of the sea, the birds of the air, and over every living creature that moves upon the earth (Gen 1:28). It was a kingdom on earth as it is in heaven.

We don't know how long Adam and Eve lived in that hedged garden under the protection of the Father. Life there was of the God-style. Adam used his words, not the sweat of his brow, to establish, subdue, and create. The earth and its bounty responded to the Word of dominion by bearing fruit. There was no sickness or pain, no lack or want. Adam and Eve cultivated the garden, maintaining order and establishing the Kingdom of God in that place.

The lion lay with the lamb, and there were no predators or prey. Every living thing of the plant and animal kingdom multiplied. The fruit of the plants were for food, and death had no dominion in that place.

The only word spoken was of the God-realm, bringing life and joy and peace, faith and gentleness and goodness, and humility and self-control to all who heard it. These are the fruits of the Spirit that dwelled and abounded in the Garden of Eden.

There was no doubt, no contention, no competition between the living things. Adam and Eve's dominion was honored and everything thrived. God walked with Adam, shared His heart and His vision for the garden and the earth, and Adam carried out God's desires with Eve at his side. It was the realm of God's glory.

Man's fruit from his womb was children; the fruit of his spirit was joy, peace, patience, faith, gentleness, goodness, humility, and self-control. Being made in the God-class, he produced the fruit of the life that manifests God's own nature.

Lucifer, the leader of the usurpers of the angelic host, wanted that headship over the earth, and we know what transpired in the garden. When Adam and Eve, our ancestors, listened to the lie of the usurper, then changed the words that

God had said to them, they exchanged the lie for the truth. When they believed and obeyed the deceiver instead of God, they forfeited their throne and were banished from their heavenly home. What is even worse is that the Spirit's life in them died, and they came under the curse of sin and death.

The fruit of the Spirit no longer abided in their hearts. The Word that brought life and peace and joy and all the other attributes of the God-race were replaced by words from the usurper.

Now his words would reign supreme in their hearts; his lies would hold dominion. The fruit of the broken and lost prisoner is death, sorrow, and despair. Now restlessness, doubt and fear replace peace, faith, and joy. Now pride and arrogance, hate, and unrestraint have dominion over humility, self-control, and benevolence or goodness. Today the battle within us rages, and the gardens of our hearts seem more like a war zone than a haven.

When our patriarchs called the lie the truth, and believed it and followed it, they not only lost their dominion, they also corrupted and polluted their nature. As their seed, we are now in their image; our nature is like theirs. Our spirit-man, which shared the identity and nature of our Father, withered because it was cut off at the root by the free choice of our first parents.

We not only inherit the physical attributes of our ancestors, we also inherit their Adamic nature. We are conceived wounded, live wounded, and our perceptions are behaviors are tainted by our Adamic nature until we are born again in Christ. Then the Holy Spirit transforms us by renewing our minds with the living Word. This is a process that begins with healing the wounded heart.

A look at Genesis 3 will provide a picture of what happened to us in the fall. We exchanged the lie for the truth, and its consequences have been far reaching. First, our fallen Adamic nature tells us that God will withhold good from us; so now we have to watch out for ourselves. We have exchanged our Father's protection and sovereignty in our lives with our own efforts.

When Eve changed the words that God said, confusion and doubt replaced rest and faith. Then folly and disaster could reign in her heart. We are born with that same corrupted nature. Therefore, we no longer trust God. Our hearts are closed to His love and His life in us. Confusion and doubt keep us out!

Eve blamed the serpent, and Adam blamed Eve. Neither would accept responsibility for their behaviors. Our Adamic nature also wants to blame or hide behind others. We don't want to look "bad." We don't want to pay the price. Now we are afraid to be caught, to be punished, or to be rejected. Because we have exchanged reverential fear for unhealthy fear, now we are afraid of God. Therefore we hide from His presence; we don't seek Him out.

The last devastating consequence of the fall is that men and women fear and distrust one another at the heart level.[7] It started when Adam blamed Eve for his treason against God. That put a wedge of distrust and suspicion between him and Eve. Eve, on the other hand, became insecure in her heart relationship with her husband. She tried to know his every thought, seeking security in the relationship. This drove a further separation between them. Our corruption began in their hearts. Distrust rules our relationships until we have a new heart.

Death, sorrow, despair, restlessness, doubt, fear, pride and arrogance, hate, and unrestraint are the fruits of the garden of the heart separated from the love and life of Jehova God. The same thing that separated Adam and Eve separates us. Missing the mark, we became self-reliant, doubting the trustworthiness of our Father. We gave the deceiver the keys to our hearts and our lives. Even believers can fall or slip back into that kingdom, sometimes unaware of the sin that took them out of the Kingdom of God. The good news is that this situation is not irreversible.

Through repentance, literally, *turning away*, can we regain the life of the Kingdom of God and intimacy with our Father. God is faithful in His covenant to us. When we lay down our life and our ways, He raises us in His life and His ways. We can now come to the garden, to the Kingdom of God, and eat of the fruits of Jesus' labors on our behalf. Those fruits are ours today by the same Holy Spirit that filled Jesus Christ at His baptism.

The fruits of the Adamic nature are in direct contrast to the fruits of the Spirit. In the Adamic nature, sorrow and fear have usurped joy and faith. We walk in a spirit of condemnation, with pride and arrogance covering up our shame and our pain. Self-reliance has replaced utter reliance upon God, and we scrap and scrape for position and the crumbs that fall from the table of the prosperous.

Patience and longsuffering have been replaced with bitterness and hardened hearts. We desire instant gratification.

Distrust reigns in the most intimate relationships. We are even wounded in the womb of our mothers before we enter the world. In the Adamic nature, the kingdom of man, safety doesn't exist, and "life is what you make it."

With each successive generation, the disparity between good and evil has become more and more apparent in our cultures. Living in the land of extremes, a change is becoming apparent. The middle ground of complacency is giving way. The fences of compromise that we have been straddling are burning, and people are either getting hungry for the things of God or hungry for self-promotion and personal gain. Those not at all hungry are left by the wayside.

In our day the media, government, and even some church arenas "push the envelope" of amorality and contempt for God. The "secular" world, the kingdom of man, is at open war with the Kingdom of God. Prayer is openly condemned and barred from schools and public congregations. Many promote removing "under God" from our Pledge of Allegiance, and "In God We Trust" from our currency. Homosexuality is a legitimate lifestyle now condoned by the government, even allowing marriage between same sexes.

As a culture, we Americans are self-serving, man-fearing, and the reverential fear of God has little or no prominent place in our academic, business, or social world. The serpent in Eden planted a seed that has taken root in the garden of our hearts. Not only have we been missing the mark, we now deny, as a culture, that a "mark" even exists. It is important to understand the roots of our corruption. Only by routing out the roots of corruption, can we eradicate the fruits of corruption.

When Adam followed the leadings of the serpent, he exchanged his position with Lucifer. He traded the fruits of the Spirit for the fruits of the lie. Death touched every living thing. The entire earth and all its inhabitants along with their seed became corrupt. We see only dimly now the former glory of the earth as it was in the garden. But there is good news!

Satan won that crown of earthly dominion, but only temporarily. Jesus Christ, the second Adam, the son of Promise, the son of God, became a man in our nature. His atonement paid the price for our full restoration to the position that Adam and Eve had forfeited by their sin. His life modeled the life of the Spirit, the life of victory and divine purpose. He told us and showed us how to walk in the fruits of the Spirit.

The deceiver's stronghold was eternally overthrown. Not only did he lose dominion over the earth, he also lost authority over us. Death lost its sting; sickness had to bow to health. Poverty gave way to prosperity. Hopelessness stooped to eternal security. In Christ we may have this victory *now*.

The *Christed* person now is seated positionally at the side of Christ in heavenly places through the power of the new birth. It is within this new creation's power to enforce the Word of God. This new man has the commission to subdue the earth and to walk in the fruits and gifts of the Spirit of God. Just as Jesus Himself did in his ministry on the earth and Adam did in the garden, the born-again *Christed* person walks in the glory and dominion of God.

To the person who has not experienced this

transformation, this sounds impossible. The world says "If it sounds too good to be true, it probably is [too good to be true]." That is the paradox of the Kingdom of God: if it sounds too good to be true, it's probably true! When God gives, He blesses abundantly, and He doesn't take His blessings back! When we open our hearts and lives to Christ, He deposits His life in us, beginning a transformation that manifests *Christness* through us.

We have all the fruits of the Spirit deposited in us when we are born again. Even as we start this new life as babes, so too, are the fruits planted as seeds. It is our divine purpose as sons of God, walking in grace, to cultivate the fruits of the Spirit that were the seeds planted into our hearts at our rebirth.

We are the tillers of the soil of our own hearts. By cultivating the garden of our hearts, tending to it with the care and diligence that characterize the commission given to the first Adam in the first garden, the fruits of the Spirit life in us will mature, and become meat for the hungry and the thirsty.

This means that we must prune our desires with self-control, weed the soil of our hearts with humility and meekness, water our minds with the Word of faith, strengthen our resolve with joy, grow in faith with patience, and tend to the new seedlings of relationships with gentleness and goodness. To try to accomplish this in our own strength would be folly. We need the grace of God operating in our lives to bring the fruits of the Holy Spirit into full harvest. Peter, in his second epistle made it plain:

> His divine power has given us everything we need
> for life and godliness through our knowledge of
> him who called us by his own glory and goodness.

Through these he has given us his very great and precious promises, so that through them you may participate in the divine nature and escape the corruption in the world caused by evil desires. For this very reason, make every effort to add to your faith goodness; and to goodness, knowledge; and to knowledge, self-control; and to self-control, perseverance; and to perseverance, godliness; and to godliness, brotherly kindness; and to brotherly kindness, love. For if you possess these qualities in increasing measure, they will keep you from being ineffective and unproductive in your knowledge of our Lord Jesus Christ. But if anyone does not have them, he is nearsighted and blind, and has forgotten that he has been cleansed from his past sins.

(2 Pet 1:3-9 NIV)

Peter here describes the consequences of both cultivating and ignoring the fruits of the Spirit: one will cause an increase in the measure of these qualities. One will bring about a decrease, causing us to become blind and fall into the old Adamic nature that promoted fear and performance. What a wonderful encouragement Peter gives us! We have been given everything that pertains to godliness. We may participate in the divine nature and escape the corruption of the world.

By cultivating the life of the Spirit in us, by increasing the fruits of love, joy, peace, longsuffering, gentleness, goodness, faith, meekness, and temperance, and bringing their growth to maturity, we participate in the divine nature by manifesting the gifts of the Spirit for the profit of all.

In addition to these "fruits of the Spirit," the Bible

describes the "gifts" or the manifestations of the Spirit. They concern our words, our thoughts, and our deeds. The utterance gifts are prophesy, divers kinds of tongues, and interpretation of tongues. The gifts of revelation are the word of knowledge, the word of wisdom, and the discerning of spirits. The gifts of power are the gift of faith, the working of miracles, and the gift of healings (1 Cor. 12:6-11). These "gifts" are the means by which we grow into spiritual maturity and fulfill the divine call in our lives.

Many have thought these gifts are no longer in operation, but I submit that the great commission has not been fulfilled, and that God has not withdrawn His Spirit nor the manifestation of His workings from us. "But all these worketh that one and the selfsame Spirit, dividing to every man severally as he will" (1 Cor. 12:11). Jesus was given the Spirit without measure, but we, too, are given the gifts of the Spirit which we will use as we develop the fruits of the life of the Spirit of God in our lives.

These gifts, however great, are not the first things. They are the result of the cultivation of the fruits of the Spirit. A *Christed* life is a life rich in nurture and nourishment. *The fruits of the Spirit are the diet of the transformed heart.* The inner man of the heart is the caretaker of a garden that produces abundance that will prosper all who partake of its fruit. It will feed one; it will feed all. "And he shall be like a tree planted by the rivers of water, that bringeth forth his fruit in his season; his leaf also shall not wither; and whatsoever he doeth shall prosper (Psa. 1:3).

Now we are the enforcers, by the power and the authority of the Name of Jesus Christ, whose God-class nature we share in brotherhood with Him under His Lordship. The dominion we were given through Adam in the garden has been reestablished by the second Adam, the last Adam, Jesus Christ. Abiding on the vine, we bear the fruit of the Spirit, which will profit all. It will profit ourselves and the peoples who eat of them as we minister to them from the love and the life of Jesus Christ.

The Fruits of the Spirit

> *We do not need to struggle to achieve them,*
> *and we do not need to pray to receive them.*
>
> *We HAVE them when the Holy Spirit makes His*
> *abode in our hearts!*
>
> > *They are the fruits of the*
> > > *yielded and transformed life,*
> > *the gifts that make us*
> > > *the fruitbearers on the vine:*
> > > *revealing agape love,*
> > *the God-kind-of-love*
> > > *to a lost and hungry world;*

RELATED SCRIPTURES (KJV)

Isa 51:3 For the LORD shall comfort Zion: he will comfort all her waste places; and he will make her wilderness like Eden, and her desert like the garden of the LORD; joy and gladness shall be found therein, thanksgiving, and the voice of melody.

Isa 58:11 And the LORD shall guide thee continually, and satisfy thy soul in drought, and make fat thy bones: and thou shalt be like a watered garden, and like a spring of water, whose waters fail not.

Deu 7:13 And he will love thee, and bless thee, and multiply thee: he will also bless the fruit of thy womb, and the fruit of thy land, thy corn, and thy wine, and thine oil, the increase of thy kine, and the flocks of thy sheep, in the land which he sware unto thy fathers to give thee.

Deu 22:9 Thou shalt not sow thy vineyard with divers seeds: lest the fruit of thy seed which thou hast sown, and the fruit of thy vineyard, be defiled.

Psa 1:3 And he shall be like a tree planted by the rivers of water, that bringeth forth his fruit in his season; his leaf also shall not wither; and whatsoever he doeth shall prosper.

Psa 92:14 They shall still bring forth fruit in old age; they shall be fat and flourishing.

Prov 8:13-14 The fear of the LORD is to hate evil: Counsel is mine, and sound wisdom: I am understanding; I have strength.
Prov 8:19 My fruit is better than gold, yea, than fine gold; and my revenue than choice silver.

Prov 11:30 The fruit of the righteous is a tree of life; and he that winneth souls is wise.

Prov 12:14 A man shall be satisfied with good by the fruit of his mouth: and the recompense of a man's hands shall be rendered unto him.

Ezek 47:12 And by the river upon the bank thereof, on this side and on that side, shall grow all trees for meat, whose leaf shall not fade, neither shall the fruit thereof be consumed: it shall bring forth new fruit according to his months, because their waters they issued out of the sanctuary: and the fruit thereof shall be for meat, and the leaf thereof for medicine.

Mal 3:11-12 And I will rebuke the devourer for your sakes, and he shall not destroy the fruits of your ground; neither shall your vine cast her fruit before the time in the field, saith the LORD of hosts. And all nations shall call you blessed: for ye shall be a delightsome land, saith the LORD of hosts.

Mat 3:10 And now also the ax is laid unto the root of the trees: therefore every tree which bringeth not forth good fruit is hewn down, and cast into the fire.

Mat 12:33 Either make the tree good, and his fruit good; or else make the tree corrupt, and his fruit corrupt: for the tree is known by his fruit.

Mat 13:8 But other fell into good ground, and brought fruit, some an hundredfold, some sixtyfold, some thirtyfold.
John 15:2 Every branch in me that beareth not fruit he taketh away: and every branch that beareth fruit, he purgeth it, that it may bring forth more fruit.

John 15:4-8 Abide in me, and I in you. As the branch cannot bear fruit of itself, except it abide in the vine; no more can ye, except ye abide in me. I am the vine, ye are the branches: He that abideth in me, and I in him, the same bringeth forth much fruit: for without me ye can do nothing. If a man abide not in me, he is cast forth as a branch, and is withered; and men gather them, and cast them into the fire, and they are burned. If ye abide in me, and my words abide in you, ye shall ask what ye will, and it shall be done unto you. Herein is my Father glorified, that ye bear much fruit; so shall ye be my disciples.

John 15:16 Ye have not chosen me, but I have chosen you, and ordained you, that ye should go and bring forth fruit, and that your fruit should remain: that whatsoever ye shall ask of the Father in my name, he may give it you.

Rom 6:22 But now being made free from sin, and become servants to God, ye have your fruit unto holiness, and the end everlasting life.

Rev 22:2 In the midst of the street of it, and on either side of the river, was there the tree of life, which bare twelve manner of fruits, and yielded her fruit every month: and the leaves of the tree were for the healing of the nations

Jesus' Mission Statement

The Spirit of the Lord is upon me,

because he hath anointed me

to preach the gospel to the poor;

he hath sent me to heal the brokenhearted,

to preach deliverance to the captives,

and recovering of sight to the blind,

to set at liberty them that are bruised,

To preach the acceptable year of the Lord.

Luke 4:18-19 (KJV)

On the tenth day of Christness,
my Lord, He gave to me

TEN HORNS A'BLOWIN'

But *Thou hast exalted my horn* like that of the wild ox; *I have been anointed with fresh oil.* (Psa. 92:10 NCV)

With trumpets and sound of cornet make a joyful noise before the LORD, the King (Psa 98:6 KJV).

There will I make the horn of David to bud: I have ordained a lamp for mine anointed (Luke 1:69 KJV).

And hath raised up *an horn of salvation* for from the family of God's servant David (Psa . 132:17 KJV).

The God of my rock; in him will I trust: he is my shield, and *the horn of my salvation*, my high tower, and my refuge, my saviour; thou savest me from violence (2 Sam. 22:3 KJV).

And Abraham lifted up his eyes, and looked, and behold behind him a *ram caught in a thicket by his horns:* and Abraham went and took the ram, and offered him *up for a burnt offering in the stead of his son* (Gen . 22:13 KJV).

And he shall put some of the blood upon the *horns of the altar* which is before the LORD, that is in the tabernacle of the congregation, and shall pour out all the blood at the bottom of the altar of the burnt offering, which is at the door of the tabernacle of the congregation (Lev. 4:18 KJV).

And it shall come to pass, that when they make a long blast with the ram's horn, and when ye hear the *sound of the trumpet,* all the people shall shout with a great shout; and the *wall of the city shall fall down flat,* and the people shall ascend up every man straight before him (Josh. 6:5 KJV).

Thou lovest righteousness, and hatest wickedness: therefore God, thy God, hath anointed thee with the *oil of gladness* above thy fellows (Psa. 45:7 KJV).

Praise him with the sound of the trumpet: praise him with the psaltery and harp (Psa. 150:3 KJV).

And he shall send his angels with a great *sound of a trumpet, and they shall gather together his elect from the four winds, from one end of heaven to the other* Matt. 24:31 KJV).

In a moment, in the twinkling of an eye, at the last trump: *for the trumpet shall sound, and the dead shall be raised incorruptible, and we shall be changed* (1 Cor. 15:52 KJV).

And I beheld, and, lo, in the midst of the throne and of the four beasts, and in the midst of the elders, stood *a Lamb as it had been slain, having seven horns and seven eyes, which are the seven Spirits of God sent forth into all the earth* (Rev. 5:6 KJV).

[all italics mine]

"

Hey, mom! Can you hear them? Can you hear them? The horns! The parade is coming! Let's get up front, mom. I don't want to miss anything. Hurry!"

"Wow, Ellen, look at the centerpiece. Isn't it just beautiful! It's a cornucopia just overflowing with fresh fruits! I wonder if that is a real animal's horn. It's just magnificent!"

"The hunt! The hunt! Blow the horns and call the riders! The hunt is on!"

"Dad, were there unicorns on the ark? What happened to them? It looked like a horse with a horn on its head. Did it have wings, too, Dad? Did it?"

"Welcome to the arena! Today we shall see the greatest matador in the country, Miguel, as he challenges the fierce horned bull in battle!"

"General, the men are ready," replied the sergeant.
"Good! Call them forth! Sound the horns! We're off to battle!"

"Hail to the King! Hail to the King!" resounded the shouts of the people as the horns announced the coming of the King.

Who can ignore horns? Horns make us think of celebrations, of gatherings for fun, for competition, and even for battle. Horns pierce the air with their sound. They can cause fear and trepidation to an enemy troop. They bring excitement and amazement to a little child.

The sounds of trumpets are so familiar to our western culture. They are traditional at all kinds of celebrations and assemblies. Parades, weddings, and holiday celebrations gather folks together with the sounding of the horns. Their brass sparkles and sends shoots of dazzling light as the sun strikes them. Their sounds pierce the air, announcing their coming. They signify that it's time to get together!

Unlike strings or woodwinds, horns can be heard from afar. Their songs proclaim the coming of something big! Can we imagine half-time at a football game without the sounds of horns, or a parade without horns heralding in something special?

The sounding of horns calls us to respond. Their song literally charges the air around us and we are changed. Our levels of expectation are raised. We begin to anticipate that something special is about to occur. Their call can bring us to realms of awe and even wonder; their shout can fill our hearts with terror. This is the paradox of the horn.

Horns and shouts have caused the fortified walls of cities

to fall and caused armies to turn on themselves in confusion and fear. The sounding of horns has caused the defeat of great armies.

Horn blowing was a significant factor in achieving victory in at least two major battles in the Old Testament. The first was the Battle of Jericho. This was the first battle fought when the Israelites arrived at the Promised Land. God gave them the land, but the people still had to walk that victory out by going to war against a very powerful city. They won that battle by doing what seemed like foolishness to us—marching silently and blowing horns!

Following Jehovah's instruction, the people marched around the city silently for seven days. The only sound that was made was the sound of seven trumpets which were blown as the procession moved. After seven days of silent marching around that great walled city, the people shouted with a great shout, the horns blew, and the walls that were wide enough for chariots to race on top fell down flat! (Joshua 6)

The blowing horns during those seven days had a profound effect on all who heard them. We can imagine that in the first days, the people of Jericho laughed and made derisive comments about the unarmed tribes that were marching around its borders.

But over the next few days, with the persistent call of the horns, fear and apprehension began to take hold in those hearts. The stories of Jehovah's interventions on behalf of His people must have touched those people of Jericho with dread. Then, at the seventh day, the Hebrews shouted altogether with a great shout, the horns blew, and the walls of the city crumbled. When the walls fell down, pandemonium broke out.

The city was utterly destroyed. Only Rahab, the harlot, and her family survived for she had aided the Hebrew spies who had come to check out the land. All the gold and silver of that city became part of the treasury of the Lord.

That battle cry created a sound that was heard for many years to come as the Hebrews took control of the lands that God had set apart for them. What alarm and trepidation must have grasped the hearts that heard the sounds of those horns as they approached the cities that resisted the Israelites.

Another important battle in which horns played a major part was Gideon's battle against the Midianites. The Midianites were like "grasshoppers" in number, with "countless camels." So many were their number it seemed like a plague of locusts which utterly consumed the land as they progressed. "Countless camels" give the sense that these enemy troops were without end. Their prior attacks on the Israelites had left the Jews impoverished, fearful, and discouraged.

God called upon Gideon to create an army of warriors. Thousands of farmers, weaponless and untried in war volunteered. Twice God reduced their size, and finally, when only three hundred remained, God was satisfied that He would be glorified in the battle.

He gave Gideon battle instructions. Gideon told the soldiers to each get clay pots, a torch, and a trumpet, which was in those days a ram's horn. He told them to scatter around the hills that surrounded the camps of the Midianites. Then at

Gideon's signal, the men were to break their clay pots, hold up their torches, blow their trumpets, and cry aloud!

Imagine the reverberating sounds that must have echoed through that valley of those countless mighty Midianite warriors. With sounds of breaking clay, lights moving all about, the evening skies suggested hosts coming upon them. And, indeed, the Bible tells the story.

> And the three companies blew the trumpets, and brake the pitchers, and held the lamps in their left hands, and the trumpets in their right hands to blow withal: and they cried, The sword of the LORD, and of Gideon. And they stood every man in his place round about the camp: and all the host ran, and cried, and fled. And the three hundred blew the trumpets, and the LORD set every man's sword against his fellow, even throughout all the host: and the host fled to Bethshittah in Zererath, and to the border of Abelmeholah, unto Tabbath.
>
> (Judg. 7:20 –22)

God had given His children the victory. The enemy had turned upon themselves in the frantic times that followed. The battle clearly was the Lord's. The sounding of the horns charged the air with the power and the presence of an Almighty God who would fight the battles of His children in their presence.

The same horns that announce battle can be used to sound the victory. These horns are usually accompanied with sounds of singing and celebration.

One of the Hebrew feasts that God instituted is called the Feast of Trumpets. More familiarly called "Rosh HaShana," this feast initiates a ten day celebration known as the Awesome Days.

Rosh HaShanah is the beginning of the biblical civil calendar, and the seventh month of the biblical religious calendar. Rosh HaShanah is referred to in the Torah as "Yom Yeruah," the day of the sounding of the shofar (a trumpet made from a ram's horn.) It is a feast calling the people to a great awakening.

For a month before the feast day, a trumpet (shofar) is blown at every morning service to warn the people to repent and return to God. Psalm 27 is recited at both the morning and evening services. It is a season that warns the people that God's judgment is about to come.[8]

The great awakening feast of Rosh HaShana has a number of meanings. Today that feast tells us to awake us to resurrection life. As believers whose life is hid in Christ, we are heralded to arise to our high calling. Ephesians 5:14 tells us to "Awake, sleeper, and arise from the dead, and Christ will shine on you." (NAS) For us, this feast is a celebration of eternal life!

Rosh HaShana is also referred to as the Day of Judgment. The Bible shows us that horn blowing is not relegated simply to the earth. There are horns in heaven, too, along with a host of other instruments. They are used to give praise to God, as well as to sound judgment. Isaiah refers to the awakening as a blast that brings in the thousand year reign of the Messiah (Isa. 12). This is echoed in the New Testament scriptures in the book of Thessalonians.

> For the Lord himself shall descend from heaven
> with a shout, with the voice of the archangel, and
> with the trump of God: and the dead in Christ
> shall rise first: Then we which are alive and
> remain shall be caught up together with them in

the clouds, to meet the Lord in the air: and so
shall we ever be with the Lord.

(1 Thes. 4:16-17 KJV)

In every aspect the sounding of the horns of Rosh
HaSahana is the awakening sound for a new day. And this
holiday marks it in every dimension. It is a birthday for the
world, for the church, for believers, and for the millennial season
of Messiah's earthly reign. The shofar is the instrument that God
ordered His people to sound as a call to the nations. That call is
getting louder and louder. Its persistence makes it hard to ignore.
This awakening is a sound of promise and fulfillment. It begins
with personally laying down our life, one day at a time, one
chamber of our heart at a time, until, by the power of His Spirit;
we are changed, literally transformed.

There's another sounding of horns that will affect the
earth and all its inhabitants, too. The book of Revelation calls
these the horns of judgment (Revelations 8-9). This will be a
terrible season on the earth, a time of purging and pain. Our
hearts melt at the thought of it. It causes us to sound the "horn of
salvation" to all who would listen to avoid that great and terrible
day.

The *Christed* heart yearns with the agape love of the
Father for the harvest of souls before this perilous time. The
power of that love of God in us will be like water to dry, parched
lips, like balm to the striving heart, like meat to the starving soul.
The power of that love will pull people out of the terrors of the
days to come.

The horns of judgment will shake the very foundations of

lives whose hearts are self-seeking, self-reliant, refusing the love and safe-haven of God. However, those who yield to the awakening of the horns of Rosh HaShana [repentance] will be found hidden in Christ when the forthcoming horns of judgment are sounded.

That triumph comes not from our labors, but by Christ's labors on our behalf. We yield; He works. Psalm 92 exalts God who causes us to triumph over our enemies. The psalmist declares that the fool and the brutish one who work evil will be scattered and destroyed, and that God will exalt the person who depends and relies upon Him. "But my horn shalt thou exalt like the horn of a unicorn. I shall be anointed with fresh oil" (Ps. 92:10 KJV).

The striking feature of the unicorn is its horn. It represents strength, power, and uniqueness. The psalmist is slathering in the joy of the Lord, identifying with the power and the strength of God as it manifests in him.

Like a wild ox, the psalmist is up for the charge, and nothing can stop him. The fresh anointing of God's presence and power in his life has engulfed him in passion and love for God. He expects and experiences victory on every side. His unfailing confidence in the abiding presence of God in his life brings continual strength and fruitfulness even into old age. This is the "horn o' plenty."

God is described as the "horn of salvation" in the Old Testament. This phrase is surrounded like others like "my high tower, my shield, my refuge," and "the God of my rock" in 2 Samuel.

By association, we see the horn here signifies strength in high places. The Hebrew definition of this word in this text also expands this idea. It states that "in addition to a literal horn (as projecting), it also includes the ideas of a corner of the altar, a peak of a mountain, a ray of light, and figuratively, power" (H7160 Strongs).

In the same passage, "salvation" refers to liberty, deliverance, prosperity, and safety (T3468, H3467 Strongs). Calling God the "horn of salvation," therefore, describes God as the powerful one in a high place Who brings everything a person needs or desires accompanied by liberty, security, and protection from enemy attack. This is a horn of blessings poured out by a loving God for those who call on Him in faith.

God gave Moses directions to build Him a tabernacle so that He could dwell in the midst of His people in the desert. In that tabernacle was a room that contained an altar upon which the blood of sacrifice was spilt as an offering for sin. This was a picture of Jesus Christ who would later be the perfect sacrifice for sin on the cross at Calvary. On that altar was a set of horns. The priests would hold these horns when they prayed. These horns were also grabbed onto by fugitives or criminals who sought sanctuary. That person was rewarded with sanctuary as long as he remained in that city. The horns brought refuge, safety, and grace to the prisoner.

Horns of a ram also brought release to Abraham who brought his son to the sacrificial altar in obedience to God. We can picture this holy man of God bringing his only son, the son of promise, to be sacrificed to the God who had demanded total obedience. Abraham believed that God would return his son to him, though he did not know how. At the last minute, as Abraham was about to slay his son, the Angel of the Lord stopped him. When Abraham looked up he saw a ram that was snagged in the thicket by his horns. This ram became the sacrifice instead.

This ram is another picture of Jesus Christ, who became a sacrifice for sin in our stead. God demanded that Abraham have enough faith in Him to offer his only son; and then God gave His only Son in his stead. The ram's horn reminds us of Jesus Christ, who not only moved in power and strength in His earthly ministry, but who also was the sacrifice for our sin. Jesus is our horn of salvation.

The Jewish calendar has a year that is called "Jubilee." It was instituted by God as a picture of Christ's atonement on our behalf. The shofar (a ram's horn) sounded the heralding of the Jubilee Year. During this year, all debts were cancelled and slaves were freed (Lev. 25:9-10) Jubilee was celebrated every fifty years. Spiritually, it refers to our freedom from the slavery of sin. Jesus is our Jubilee. He is the horn of our salvation!

Finally, the book of Revelations mentions the seven horns of the Spirit of God sent forth into all the earth. This passage reminds us that Jesus sits on the throne, and that the Holy Spirit is sent to the earth to guide, comfort, and lead us to Christ. It is this same Spirit who dwells in our hearts. He brings to us eternal life and intimacy with God. He manifests through us in signs and wonders accompanying the preaching of the Word to touch the hearts of those hurting and lost.

Horns are sounded to give God praise, not only on earth, but also in the heavens! Joy has the effect of creating sounds of praise. Shouts, laughter, and a great deal of horn blowing are not uncommon where joy abounds.

Who can ignore the blowing of so many horns? Even one or two horns, rightly blown, can make me jump out of my skin! Horns make us think of majesty, of war, of celebration, of angels, and of plenty. God gave us horns for announcing, for anointing, for sacrifice, for sanctuary, for salvation, for judgment, and for praise. Not only do horns signify power, strength, safety, refuge, and sacrifice, they also are instruments used to gather the peoples and even angels together as God reveals His character, His plans, and His purpose. The blowing of horns can create quite a stir. Let us not be caught unprepared when God's horns blow.

RELATED SCRIPTURES (KJV)

Josh 6:5 And it shall come to pass, that when they make a long blast with the ram's horn, and when ye hear the sound of the trumpet, all the people shall shout with a great shout; and the wall of the city shall fall down flat, and the people shall ascend up every man straight before him.

1 Sam 2:1 And Hannah prayed, and said, My heart rejoiceth in the LORD, mine horn is exalted in the LORD: my mouth is enlarged over mine enemies; because I rejoice in thy salvation

1 Sam 2:10 The adversaries of the LORD shall be broken to pieces; out of heaven shall he thunder upon them: the LORD shall judge the ends of the earth; and he shall give strength unto his king, and exalt the horn of his anointed.

2 Sam 22:3 The God of my rock; in him will I trust: he is my shield, and the horn of my salvation, my high tower, and my refuge, my saviour; thou savest me from violence.

Psa 18:2 The LORD is my rock, and my fortress, and my deliverer; my God, my strength, in whom I will trust; my buckler, and the horn of my salvation, and my high tower.

Psa 92:10 But my horn shalt thou exalt like the horn of an unicorn: I shall be anointed with fresh oil.

Dan 7:21-22 I beheld, and the same horn made war with the saints, and prevailed against them; Until the Ancient of days came, and judgment was given to the saints of the most High; and the time came that the saints possessed the kingdom

Gen 22:13 And Abraham lifted up his eyes, and looked, and behold behind him a ram caught in a thicket by his horns: and

Abraham went and took the ram, and offered him up for a burnt offering in the stead of his son.

1 Kings 1:51 And it was told Solomon, saying, Behold, Adonijah feareth king Solomon: for, lo, he hath caught hold on the horns of the altar, saying, Let king Solomon swear unto me to day that he will not slay his servant with the sword.

Num 10:9 And if ye go to war in your land against the enemy that oppresseth you, then ye shall blow an alarm with the trumpets; and ye shall be remembered before the LORD your God, and ye shall be saved from your enemies.

Psa 98:6 With trumpets and sound of cornet make a joyful noise before the LORD, the King.

Rev 8:2 And I saw the seven angels which stood before God; and to them were given seven trumpets.

Rev 5:6 And I beheld, and, lo, in the midst of the throne and of the four beasts, and in the midst of the elders, stood a Lamb as it had been slain, having seven horns and seven eyes, which are the seven Spirits of God sent forth into all the earth.

Psalm 27

The LORD is my light and my salvation; whom shall I fear? The LORD is the strength of my life; of whom shall I be afraid?

When the wicked, even mine enemies and my foes, came upon me to eat up my flesh, they stumbled and fell. Though an host should encamp against me, my heart shall not fear: though war should rise against me, in this will I be confident.

One thing have I desired of the LORD, that will I seek after; that I may dwell in the house of the LORD all the days of my life, to behold the beauty of the LORD, and to enquire in his temple.

For in the time of trouble he shall hide me in his pavilion: in the secret of his tabernacle shall he hide me; he shall set me up upon a rock. And now shall mine head be lifted up above mine enemies round about me: therefore will I offer in his tabernacle sacrifices of joy; I will sing, yea, I will sing praises unto the LORD.

Hear, O LORD, when I cry with my voice: have mercy also upon me, and answer me. When thou saidst, Seek ye my face; my heart said unto thee, Thy face, LORD, will I seek.

Hide not thy face far from me; put not thy servant away in anger: thou hast been my help; leave me not, neither forsake me, O God of my salvation. When my father and my mother forsake me, then the LORD will take me up.

Teach me thy way, O LORD, and lead me in a plain path, because of mine enemies. Deliver me not over unto the will of mine enemies: for false witnesses are risen up against me, and such as breathe out cruelty.

I had fainted, unless I had believed to see the goodness of the LORD in the land of the living. Wait on the LORD: be of good courage, and he shall strengthen thine heart: wait, I say, on the LORD. (KJV)

On the eleventh day of Christness,
My Lord, He gave to me

ELEVEN
NEW BIRTH BLESSINGS

"Eleven" sounds like "a lot" to me. In my pre-school years, learning to count from one to ten and learning the letters of the alphabet was the primary thing. That accomplishment was a milestone for me. Now I was ready for bigger and better things. That's the significance of "eleven" to me.

It's like graduating from kindergarten. Now, I thought, I am going to the big kid's school, and I will do things that the big kids do! Now I can read and write and do math! I feel so much older and more mature! I am in the big league now!

That's how "eleven" sounds to me still! It's not a quantity as much as it is a new plateau, a new level. It implies that some firm foundations have been established, foundations which will keep me secure as I move into the new discoveries ahead of me. It means that the primary things are settled and established in my head and my heart. These are the tools that I will use at every level or plateau I come upon in my life.

Knowing the alphabet and the counting numbers one through ten mean that I have the tools to read and write with understanding and that I have the tools to compute numbers and solve mathematical problems.

Knowing Jesus Christ as my personal Lord and Savior

means that I have the foundations of a new life established in my heart and forever sealed by the Holy Spirit of promise. I am born again. I know that I will live with Jesus forever and that He paid the price for my sins. I know that God is my Father and that the Holy Spirit is my Comforter and my Guide. I believe this with my heart, even though I may not understand it with my mind. I have the tools now to grow into a mature Christian.

When I was a new-born Christian I had to be fed the milk of the Word of God. The children of Israel who followed Moses out of Egypt through the desert for forty years were fed by God every day with "angel food," or "manna" as they called it. Every morning this bread from heaven was collected from the ground. They were only to collect what they needed for that day, except on the day before the Sabbath; on that day they collected enough manna for two days. If they did not eat it all and tried to save it for the next day, the manna would spoil. God wanted daily reliance from His children.

The Israelites did not have to work or struggle for their daily bread on their way to the Promised Land. God provided for every person. In fact, their shoes or clothing never wore out, and no one ever suffered with sickness! God provided *everything* they needed for the trip.

When I was first born again, God provided my spiritual food every day. I didn't have to labor for it, and I could eat it without having to prepare it. I didn't know "how" to study God's Word and I didn't know how to pray. I didn't know how to hear from God. I just knew that God heard my cry and that He cared.

If I needed something, I got it! It was so easy to hear

from God. He was at my "beck and call." If I was hurt, He took care of me. If I was hungry, He fed me. If I was sick, He healed me. If I was lonely, He filled me. If I was curious, He showed me. If I was weary, He sheltered me and gave me rest. The Bible became my most intimate companion. I couldn't wait to hear what God had to say to me next! Every word was like water for a dried-up brook, like bread for a starving person.

I didn't have to put out any effort in those early days. Nor did God expect it of me. He knows that babies need lots and lots of attention from their moms and dads. Psalm 91 shows us that God is not only our Almighty Father, but also our nursing mother. That is the meaning of "El Shaddai," the person of whom the psalm is speaking. God, our eternal Father and Mother, is committed to our well-being. He is faithful and generous with His love and His blessings. His love is deeply personal and ever available to anyone who calls on Him in faith.

After we have nursed on the milk of God's love and God's word, it is time to grow on to maturity. This means that we will have to enter the "school of the Spirit," and allow the Holy Spirit to have His way in our lives. The Holy Spirit brings us into the full revelation of Jesus Christ. While He is transforming us into Jesus Christ's image, the Holy Spirit is empowering us to fulfill the great commission with Jesus as our head. We'll have to dig a little deeper, walk in faith a little farther, and trust in His ability all the way!

God is faithful, and He is more than able to do this work through us. In fact, if He didn't do the work in us, then we would not experience the transformation power of His salvation in our lives. Our personal efforts would just add up to another dead "work" which would have no eternal value. What is born of the Spirit is nurtured and completed by the Spirit. Our part is to be sensitive to His direction, and to cooperate by obedience and trust in Him. It is *not* our job to be "in charge" of our lives. As we have known Jesus as Savior, we will now learn to know Him as Lord, or "boss."

Just as a plant has everything it needs to become mature and strong in the seed of that plant, so it is with us when we are born again. The integrity of the seed, its ability to reproduce after its own kind, is not dependent upon the environment in which it abides. The same principle is true with our new man identity as well.

When God recreates our spirit, He deposits in us everything we lost in the fall. He recreates our spirit in the God-class, the very same nature as Jesus, with the same potential for growth and maturity and reproduction. To assure that His perfect will for us would be accomplished, He gave us His own abiding presence and power in the person of the Holy Spirit. He began the work of transformation in us, and He promises to complete it, too.

When we are born again, our spirit is made alive again in the image and likeness of God. We have been made new again, just as we were in Adam and Eve before sin. God sees us whole, holy, and worthy of His love. We are His children, and we can run to His arms anytime without fear. We have been justified by the atonement of Jesus Christ. Our lives now hid in Christ, it is as if we had never sinned in the Father's eyes. He made the way for us to be restored to intimacy with Him

The Bible says that we must "work out our salvation with fear and trembling" (Phil 2:12. Even though our spirit is totally redeemed and recreated to its original nature, our soul and our physical body are not.

Working here is not a matter of "taking the bull by the horns" and overcoming by our own power. It is not "putting our shoulder to the wheel" and striving. Just as "work" in the natural realm refers to self effort, "work" in the supernatural world of God is really an exercise of faith. It is about "letting" or "allowing" God to influence and lead our hearts on the journey that will transform us into His own image. The Holy Spirit is the abiding presence in our lives Who teaches us, convicts us, corrects us, and empowers us. Our yielded heart hears and obeys in faith.

His methods are gentle, loving, and merciful. The changes come one day at a time, one line at a time, one chamber of our heart at a time. As we learn to hear Him and trust Him, we can obey Him out of love, not fear.

Our motivations change because one chamber at a time, our hearts have been cleansed and made healthy and whole. The stones of self-defense and self-protection are washed away, and "the heart of flesh" is revived. In those areas which we have yielded to Him, we are fired up with His life-giving power. I sometimes call it "God's liquid love."

The good news is that God Himself is the healer and the builder and the restorer (Heb. 5). In this walk, we are learning to trust God and to follow His ways rather than our own. It is a process that often requires patience together with faith. He must become the protector of our hearts and our lives, and that kind of "letting go" of our lives is a day-to-day process!

Finally, our physical body is also going to manifest this new birth. That process involves two time zones, the present and the future.

Religion (man's attempt to reach God) says that we must work to achieve a heavenly home, that "in this world we shall have struggles." Jesus Himself admits this is true. But in the very next phrase, the Word says, to rejoice and believe! "These things I have spoken to you, that in Me you may have peace. In the world you will have tribulation; but be of good cheer, I have overcome the world" (John 16:33 NKJV).

When we are born again of the Spirit, our lives are now hidden in Christ Himself. We have literally been translated from one kingdom to another. Our choices determine which kingdom we will live in. We can either be ruled by our self-serving minds and will, or we can submit to the rule of the Spirit of God in us.

God through Jesus Christ has provided for us all that we will ever require for an abundant life. That abundance is for *now, today*. This is the *immediate* inheritance that each believer is entitled to receive. In addition, we are promised a resurrection of our physical bodies when Christ returns to the earth. Just as He is, so we become.

All this and more is part of the new birth inheritance and blessing. Because the Bible makes it so "plain," that is, easy to understand, and because we are now in a process of greater and greater reliance upon God and His Word, Jesus Christ, I am presenting the "eleven new birth blessings" in a different format than we have been following so far in our twelve day journey.

My desire is that you, the reader, shall absorb the magnitude of God's love and His provision as you read for yourself His life-filled Word as we continue to explore the blessings of the new birth. Though the list is by no means complete, it begins to form a picture of our new identity as God Himself sees us. I believe that this revelation will change the way we see ourselves and the way that we live *now*.

> But as it is written: "Eye has not seen, nor ear heard, Nor have entered into the heart of man The things which God has prepared for those who love Him. "But God has revealed them to us through His Spirit. For the Spirit searches all things, yes, the deep things of God.

> For what man knows the things of a man except the spirit of the man which is in him? Even so no one knows the things of God except the Spirit of God. ***Now*** *we have received, not the spirit of the world, but the Spirit who is from God, that we might know the things that have been freely given to us by God.*

> These things we also speak, not in words which man's wisdom teaches but which the Holy Spirit teaches, comparing spiritual things with spiritual. But the natural man does not receive the things of the Spirit of God, for they are foolishness to him; nor can he know them, because they are spiritually discerned.
> 1 Cor. 2: 9-14 (NKJV) *(italics mine)*

New Birth Blessing #1

I am a new creation with a new nature. It is the nature of Jesus and of God the Father because Jesus and I have made the great exchange--His life for mine, my old life for His. It is the gift of God which I accept by faith.

(Rom 8:29 NIV) For those God foreknew he also predestined to be conformed to the likeness of his Son, that he might be the firstborn among many brothers.

(Rom 14:8 KJV) For whether we live, we live unto the Lord; and whether we die, we die unto the Lord: whether we live therefore, or die, we are the Lord's.

(1 Cor 3:16 KJV) Know ye not that ye are the temple of God, and that the Spirit of God dwelleth in you?

(Col 2:11-14 NLT) When you came to Christ, you were "circumcised," but not by a physical procedure. It was a spiritual procedure--the cutting away of your sinful nature. For you were buried with Christ when you were baptized. And with him you were raised to a new life because you trusted the mighty power of God, who raised Christ from the dead. You were dead because of your sins and because your sinful nature was not yet cut away. Then God made you alive with Christ. He forgave all our sins. He canceled the record that contained the charges against us. He took it and destroyed it by nailing it to Christ's cross.

(Gal 3:13 NCV) Christ took away the curse the law put on us. He changed places with us and put himself under that curse.

(Rom 6:3-6 KJV) Know ye not, that so many of us as were baptized into Jesus Christ were baptized into his death? Therefore we are buried with him by baptism into death: that like as Christ was raised up from the dead by the glory of the Father, even so we also should walk in newness of life. For if we have been planted together in the likeness of his death, we shall be also in the likeness of his resurrection: Knowing this, that our old man is crucified with him, that the body of sin might be destroyed, that henceforth we should not serve sin.

(Eph 2:6 KJV) And God raised us up with Christ and seated us with him in the heavenly realms in Christ Jesus.

(Eph 2:8 KJV) For by grace are ye saved through faith; and that not of yourselves: it is the gift of God.

(Eph 2:10 NIV) For we are God's workmanship, created in Christ Jesus to do good works, which God prepared in advance for us to do.

(Rom 8:11 NIV) And if the Spirit of him who raised Jesus from the dead is living in you, he who raised Christ from the dead will also give life to your mortal bodies through his Spirit, who lives in you.

(Titus 3:5-7 NCV) he saved us because of his mercy. It was not because of good deeds we did to be right with him. He saved us through the washing that made us new people through the Holy Spirit. God poured out richly upon us that Holy Spirit through Jesus Christ our Savior. Being made right with God by his grace, we could have the hope of receiving the life that never ends.

(1 Cor 2:12 KJV) Now we have received, not the spirit of the world, but the spirit which is of God; that we might know the things that are freely given to us of God.

(2 Cor 5:21 NIV) God made him who had no sin to be sin for us, so that in him we might become the righteousness of God.

(Col 2:10 KJV) And ye are complete in him, which is the head of all principality and power:

(Col 3:1 NIV) Since, then, you have been raised with Christ, set your hearts on things above, where Christ is seated at the right hand of God.

(Rom 8:29 NIV)   For those God foreknew he also predestined to be conformed to the likeness of his Son, that he might be the firstborn among many brothers.

(Rom 14:8 KJV)   For whether we live, we live unto the Lord; and whether we die, we die unto the Lord: whether we live therefore, or die, we are the Lord's.

(1 Cor 3:16 KJV)   Know ye not that ye are the temple of God, and that the Spirit of God dwelleth in you?

(1 John 4:8-9 NIV) Whoever does not love does not know God, because God is love. This is how God showed his love among us: He sent his one and only Son into the world that we might live through him.

(2 Pet 1:4 KJV)   Through these he has given us his very great and precious promises, so that through them you may participate in the divine nature and escape the corruption in the world caused by evil desires.

New Birth Blessing #2

I am a true child of God now because I have the same nature as Jesus. The Father calls me His son or daughter; I call Him Abba, Dad. I belong to a family that it will take an eternity to know and love personally! Traditions and doctrines didn't bring us together— rather, they separated us. Now I will always know where and to whom I belong!

(Rom 8:16 KJV) The Spirit itself beareth witness with our spirit, that we are the children of God:

(Rom 8:14 KJV) For as many as are led by the Spirit of God, they are the sons of God.

(1 John 5:19 NIV) We know that we are children of God, and that the whole world is under the control of the evil one.

(Rom 8:16 KJV) The Spirit itself beareth witness with our spirit, that we are the children of God:

(Rom 8:15 KJV) For ye have not received the spirit of bondage again to fear; but ye have received the Spirit of adoption, whereby we cry, Abba, Father.

(Eph 1:5-6 NKJV) having predestined us to adoption as sons by Jesus Christ to Himself, according to the good pleasure of His will, to the praise of the glory of His grace, by which He has made us accepted in the Beloved.

(John 1:12 KJV) But as many as received him, to them gave he power to become the sons of God, even to them that believe on his name:

(Gal 4:6 KJV) And because ye are sons, God hath sent forth the Spirit of his Son into your hearts, crying, Abba, Father.

(Mark 3:35 KJV) For whosoever shall do the will of God, the same is my brother, and my sister, and mother.

(Gal 3:29 KJV) And if ye be Christ's, then are ye Abraham's seed, and heirs according to the promise.

(Ps.23:6 KJV) Surely goodness and mercy shall follow me all the days of my life and I shall dwell in the house of the LORD forever.

(Mark 10:29-39 KJV) And Jesus answered and said, Verily I say unto you, There is no man that hath left house, or brethren, or sisters, or father, or mother, or wife, or children, or lands, for my sake, and the gospel's, But he shall receive an hundredfold now in this time, houses, and brethren, and sisters, and mothers, and children, and lands, with persecutions; and in the world to come eternal life.

(John 3:15 KJV) That whosoever believeth in him should not perish, but have eternal life.

(Mat 18:21-22 KJV) Then came Peter to him, and said, Lord, how oft shall my brother sin against me, and I forgive him? till seven times? Jesus saith unto him, I say not unto thee, Until seven times: but, Until seventy times seven.

(Phil. 1:15-16 KJV) For perhaps he therefore departed for a season, that thou shouldest receive him for ever; Not now as a servant, but above a servant, a brother beloved, specially to me, but how much more unto thee, both in the flesh, and in the Lord?

(1 John 3:14 KJV) We know that we have passed from death unto life, because we love the brethren. He that loveth not his brother abideth in death.

(John 10:16 KJV) And other sheep I have, which are not of this fold: them also I must bring, and they shall hear my voice; and there shall be one fold, and one shepherd.

(John 17:21-23 KJV) That they all may be one; as thou, Father, art in me, and I in thee, that they also may be one in us: that the world may believe that thou hast sent me. And the glory which thou gavest me I have given them; that they may be one, even as we are one: I in them, and thou in me, that they may be made perfect in one; and that the world may know that thou hast sent me, and hast loved them, as thou hast loved me.

New Birth Blessing #3

I am loved by God unconditionally. He can't love me any more than He does now. In Christ I am righteous before a just God. Because Jesus' blood washes my sin and old sin nature away, that means my Father sees me clean and pure, as if I had never sinned! Jesus has become my sponsor. He is my Savior and Lord. I come into my Father's presence with confidence and assurance that He will welcome me, hear me, and answer my prayer.

(Luke 12:32 KJV) Fear not, little flock; for it is your Father's good pleasure to give you the kingdom.

(Rom 11:29 KJV) For the gifts and calling of God are without repentance.

(Rom 11:29 NCV) God never changes his mind about the people he calls and the things he gives them.

John 3:16 NCV) "God loved the world so much that he gave his one and only Son so that whoever believes in him may not be lost, but have eternal life.

(John 17:23 NCV) I will be in them and you will be in me so that they will be completely one. Then the world will know that you sent me and that you loved them just as much as you loved me. [Jesus praying to our Father]

(Rom 3:22 KJV) Even the righteousness of God which is by faith of Jesus Christ unto all and upon all them that believe: for there is no difference:

(Rom 3:25 KJV) Whom God hath set forth to be a propitiation through faith in his blood, to declare his righteousness for the remission of sins that are past, through the forbearance of God;

(Rom 4:5-6 NIV) However, to the man who does not work but trusts God who justifies the wicked, his faith is credited as righteousness. David says the same thing when he speaks of the blessedness of the man to whom God credits righteousness apart from works:

(Rom 5:19 KJV) For as by one man's disobedience many were made sinners, so by the obedience of one shall many be made righteous.

(Rom 1:17 KJV) For in the gospel a righteousness from God is revealed, a righteousness that is by faith from first to last, just as it is written: "The righteous will live by faith."

(Rom 10:4 NIV) Christ is the end of the law so that there may be righteousness for everyone who believes.

(Rom 10:10 KJV) For with the heart man believeth unto righteousness; and with the mouth confession is made unto salvation.

(2 Cor 5:21 NIV) God made him who had no sin to be sin for us, so that in him we might become the righteousness of God.

(Eph 4:24 KJV) And that ye put on the new man, which after God is created in righteousness and true holiness.

(Phil 3:9 NIV) and be found in him, not having a righteousness of my own that comes from the law, but that which is through faith in Christ--the righteousness that comes from God and is by faith.

(1 Pet 2:24 NIV) He himself bore our sins in his body on the tree, so that we might die to sins and live for righteousness; by his wounds you have been healed.

(1 John 5:14 KJV) And this is the confidence that we have in him, that, if we ask any thing according to his will, he heareth us:

(1 John 5:15 KJV) And if we know that he hear us, whatsoever we ask, we know that we have the petitions that we desired of him.

(John 16:23-24 KJV) And in that day ye shall ask me nothing. Verily, verily, I say unto you, Whatsoever ye shall ask the Father in my name, he will give it you. Hitherto have ye asked nothing in my name: ask, and ye shall receive, that your joy may be full.

(John 15:7 KJV) If ye abide in me, and my words abide in you, ye shall ask what ye will, and it shall be done unto you.

New Birth Blessing # 4

As my Father's legitimate child, I am an heir to all His estate. That estate is all of God's promises in the Bible. They are mine to enjoy now and for all eternity. His promises are for today! Jesus said the Kingdom of Heaven has come NOW, on this earth and in this time. His Kingdom has everything I'll ever need for victory.

(Gal 3:9 NLT) And so it is: All who put their faith in Christ share the same blessing Abraham received because of his faith.

(2 Pet 1:4 KJV) Whereby are given unto us exceeding great and precious promises: that by these ye might be partakers of the divine nature, having escaped the corruption that is in the world through lust

(Heb 6:12 KJV) That ye be not slothful, but followers of them who through faith and patience inherit the promises.

(Luke 12:32 KJV) Fear not, little flock; for it is your Father's good pleasure to give you the kingdom.

(1 Cor 2:12 KJV) Now we have received, not the spirit of the world, but the spirit which is of God; that we might know the things that are freely given to us of God.

(Acts 2:39 KJV) For the promise is unto you, and to your children, and to all that are afar off, even as many as the Lord our God shall call.

(Acts 16:31 KJV) And they said, Believe on the Lord Jesus Christ, and thou shalt be saved, and thy house.

(Mat 19:29 KJV) And every one that hath forsaken houses, or brethren, or sisters, or father, or mother, or wife, or children, or lands, for my name's sake, shall receive an hundredfold, and shall inherit everlasting life.

(2 Cor 1:20 KJV) For all the promises of God in him are yea and in him Amen unto the glory of God by us.

(Eph 1:3 KJV) Blessed be the God and Father of our Lord Jesus Christ, who hath blessed us with all spiritual blessings in heavenly places in Christ:

(John 16:23 KJV) And in that day ye shall ask me nothing. Verily, verily, I say unto you, Whatsoever ye shall ask the Father in my name, he will give it you.

(1 Cor 3:21 KJV) Therefore let no man glory in men. For all things are yours;

(2 Cor 9:8 KJV) And God is able to make all grace abound toward you; that ye, always having all sufficiency in all things, may abound to every good work:

(John 14:13 KJV) And whatsoever ye shall ask in my name, that will I do, that the Father may be glorified in the Son.

(John 14:14 KJV) If ye shall ask any thing in my name, I will do it.

New Birth Blessing #5

I am empowered with the vision of God's personal involvement in every aspect of my life. (Yes, I am that important to Him.) I am God's fruit bearer on this earth. He gave me the keys! He must really trust me! He said He is the vine, and I am the branch. (That's the part with the fruit.) I'm not crazy about the pruning part, but the yield far exceeds anything my puny efforts could produce. He has a plan for my life, a plan to prosper me and not to harm me, a plan to give me a hope and a future.

(Luke 15:4 KJV) What man of you, having an hundred sheep, if he lose one of them, doth not leave the ninety and nine in the wilderness, and go after that which is lost, until he find it?

(Jer 1:5 KJV) Before I formed thee in the belly I knew thee; and before thou camest forth out of the womb I sanctified thee, and I ordained thee a prophet unto the nations.

(Mat 6:30-33 NIV) If that is how God clothes the grass of the field, which is here today and tomorrow is thrown into the fire, will he not much more clothe you, O you of little faith? So do not worry, saying, 'What shall we eat?' or 'What shall we drink?' or 'What shall we wear?' For the pagans run after all these things, and your heavenly Father knows that you need them. But seek first his kingdom and his righteousness, and all these things will be given to you as well.

(Mat 10:30 KJV) But the very hairs of your head are all numbered.

(2 Tim 2:19 NIV) Nevertheless, God's solid foundation stands firm, sealed with this inscription: "The Lord knows those who are his," and, "Everyone who confesses the name of the Lord must turn away from wickedness."

(Jer 29:11 KJV) For I know the thoughts that I think toward you, saith the LORD, thoughts of peace, and not of evil, to give you an expected end.

(1 Cor 2:9 KJV) But as it is written, Eye hath not seen, nor ear heard, neither have entered into the heart of man, the things which God hath prepared for them that love him.
(Luke 10:19 KJV) Behold, I give unto you power to tread on serpents and scorpions, and over all the power of the enemy: and nothing shall by any means hurt you.

(Rom 8:28 KJV) And we know that all things work together for good to them that love God, to them who are the called according to his purpose.

(Phil 1:6 KJV) Being confident of this very thing, that he which hath begun a good work in you will perform it until the day of Jesus Christ:

(Mat 6:8 KJV) Be not ye therefore like unto them: for your Father knoweth what things ye have need of, before ye ask him.

(John 15:1-3 KJV) I am the true vine, and My Father is the vinedresser. Every branch in Me that does not bear fruit He takes away;[1] and every branch that bears fruit He prunes, that it may bear more fruit. You are already clean because of the word which I have spoken to you.

(John 15:4-5 KJV) Abide in me, and I in you. As the branch cannot bear fruit of itself, except it abide in the vine; no more can ye, except ye abide in me. I am the vine, ye are the branches: He that abideth in me, and I in him, the same bringeth forth much fruit: for without me ye can do nothing.

(John 15:8 KJV) Herein is my Father glorified, that ye bear much fruit; so shall ye be my disciples.

(John 15:16 KJV) Ye have not chosen me, but I have chosen you, and ordained you, that ye should go and bring forth fruit, and that your fruit should remain: that whatsoever ye shall ask of the Father in my name, he may give it you.

(Mat 7:16-18 KJV) Ye shall know them by their fruits. Do men gather grapes of thorns, or figs of thistles? Even so every good tree bringeth forth good fruit; but a corrupt tree bringeth forth evil fruit. A good tree cannot bring forth evil fruit, neither can a corrupt tree bring forth good fruit.

(Rev 3:19 KJV) As many as I love, I rebuke and chasten: be zealous therefore, and repent.

(Eph 1:4-5 KJV) For he chose us in him before the creation of the world to be holy and blameless in his sight. In love he predestined us to be adopted as his sons through Jesus Christ, in accordance with his pleasure and will--

(Phil 3:14 KJV) I press toward the mark for the prize of the high calling of God in Christ Jesus.

(Phil 1:6 KJV) Being confident of this very thing, that he which hath begun a good work in you will perform it until the day of Jesus Christ:

(Heb 10:35 KJV) Cast not away therefore your confidence, which hath great recompense of reward.

(Luke 12:30-32 KJV) For all these things do the nations of the world seek after: and your Father knoweth that ye have need of these things. But rather seek ye the kingdom of God; and all these things shall be added unto you. Fear not, little flock; for it is your Father's good pleasure to give you the kingdom.

New Birth Blessing #6

I am lead by inner peace, and fear has no power over me. The Spirit of God lives in me. He is my guide and teacher. My circumstances cannot dictate my life any longer. Christ defeated Satan at the cross. Now I walk by faith and not by sight. His grace is sufficient for every need. I can grow in the confidence that where He leads, He feeds, and where He guides, He provides. He is my Waymaker.

(2 Tim 1:7 AMP) For God did not give us a spirit of timidity (of cowardice, of craven and cringing and fawning fear), but [He has given us a spirit] of power and of love and of calm *and* well-balanced mind *and* discipline *and* self-control.

(Isa 41:40 KJV) Fear thou not; for I *am* with thee; be not dismayed; for I *am* thy God; I will strengthen thee; yea, I will help thee; yea, I will uphold thee with the right hand of my righteousness.

(Col 2:15 NIV) And having disarmed the powers and authorities, he made a public spectacle of them, triumphing over them by the cross.

(Rev 1:17 –18 NIV) When I saw him, I fell at his feet as though dead. Then he placed his right hand on me and said: "Do not be afraid. I am the First and the Last. I am the Living One; I was dead, and behold I am alive for ever and ever! And I hold the keys of death and Hades.

(Col 1:13 NIV) For he has rescued us from the dominion of darkness and brought us into the kingdom of the Son he loves,

(Heb 2:14 NIV) Since the children have flesh and blood, he too shared in their humanity so that by his death he might destroy him who holds the power of death--that is, the devil--

(Rom 6:14 KJV) For sin shall not have dominion over you: for ye are not under the law, but under grace.

(Heb 4:9-10 KJV) There remaineth therefore a rest to the people of God. For he that is entered into his rest, he also hath ceased from his own works, as God did from his.

(John 16:33 KJV) These things I have spoken unto you, that in me ye might have peace. In the world ye shall have tribulation:

but be of good cheer; I have overcome the world.

(Col 3:15 KJV) And let the peace of God rule in your hearts, to the which also ye are called in one body; and be ye thankful.

(John 14:27 KJV) Peace I leave with you, my peace I give unto you: not as the world giveth, give I unto you. Let not your heart be troubled, neither let it be afraid.

(John 14:26 KJV) But the Comforter, which is the Holy Ghost,whom the Father will send in my name, he shall teach you all things, and bring all things to your remembrance, whatsoever I have said unto you.

(John 6:63 NIV) The Spirit gives life; the flesh counts for nothing. The words I have spoken to you are spirit and they are life.

(Rom 8:26b KJV) but the Spirit itself maketh intercession for us with groanings which cannot be uttered.

(Rom 5:5 NIV) And hope does not disappoint us, because God has poured out his love into our hearts by the Holy Spirit, whom he has given us.

(Rom 8:6 NIV) The mind of sinful man is death, but the mind controlled by the Spirit is life and peace;

(2 Cor 1:22 NIV) [He] set his seal of ownership on us, and put his Spirit in our hearts as a deposit, guaranteeing what is to come.
(Phil 4:19 NIV) And my God will meet all your needs according to his glorious riches in Christ Jesus.

(1 John 3:21 KJV) Beloved, if our heart condemn us not, then have we confidence toward God.

New Birth Blessing #7

I don't have to earn God's approval by my good works. Jesus lived the perfect life and made the perfect sacrifice for sin, and He did it for me. That settles the account that Justice demanded. I have every legal right to God's presence and His covenant and promises. I now enjoy wholeness and wellness by grace (God's unmerited favor to me.) God sees me without sin because of the blood Jesus offered on my behalf. My past does not determine my future. I am really free from the old bonds that kept me from success. I am worthy.

(Rom 8:33 KJV) Who shall lay any thing to the charge of God's elect? It is God that justifieth.

(Titus 3:7 KJV) That being justified by his grace, we should be made heirs according to the hope of eternal life.

(Rom 3:28 KJV) Therefore we conclude that a man is justified by faith without the deeds of the law.

(Luke 18:13-14 NIV) "But the tax collector stood at a distance. He would not even look up to heaven, but beat his breast and said, 'God, have mercy on me, a sinner.' "I tell you that this man, rather than the other, went home justified before God. For everyone who exalts himself will be humbled, and he who humbles himself will be exalted."

(Acts 13:38-39 NIV) "Therefore, my brothers, I want you to know that through Jesus the forgiveness of sins is proclaimed to you. Through him everyone who believes is justified from everything you could not be justified from by the law of Moses.

(Gal 2:16 KJV) Knowing that a man is not justified by the works of the law, but by the faith of Jesus Christ, even we have believed in Jesus Christ, that we might be justified by the faith of Christ, and not by the works of the law: for by the works of the law shall no flesh be justified.

(Gal 3:11 NKJV) But that no one is justified by the law in the sight of God is evident, for "the just shall live by faith."

(1 Cor 1:8 KJV) Who shall also confirm you unto the end, that ye may be blameless in the day of our Lord Jesus Christ.

(Rom 4:9 KJV) Cometh this blessedness then upon the circumcision only, or upon the uncircumcision also? for we say that faith was reckoned to Abraham for righteousness.

(Rom 5:1-2 NIV) Therefore being justified by faith, we have peace with God through our Lord Jesus Christ: By whom also we have access by faith into this grace wherein we stand, and rejoice in hope of the glory of God.

(Eph 2:8-9 KJV) For by grace are ye saved through faith; and that not of yourselves: it is the gift of God: Not of works, lest any man should boast.

(Rom 8:1 KJV) There is therefore now no condemnation to them which are in Christ Jesus, who walk not after the flesh, but after the Spirit.

(Rom 10:10–12 NIV) For it is with your heart that you believe and are justified, and it is with your mouth that you confess and are saved. As the Scripture says, "Anyone who trusts in him will never be put to shame." For there is no difference between Jew and Gentile--the same Lord is Lord of all and richly blesses all who call on him.

(2 Cor 3:17 KJV) Now the Lord is that Spirit: and where the Spirit of the Lord is, there is liberty.

New Birth Blessing #8

I really can do all things through Christ. He has empowered me. I have authority over evil powers that come against me by the Name of Jesus Who abides in me. Jesus said that I would do everything He did in His earthly ministry and even more than that! He has made me His ambassador and the executor of His will. I am in partnership with the Holy Spirit who backs up God's word as I speak it in faith. God made no provision for failure for me. He is committed to my growth and success for His glory.

(2 Cor 3:5 KJV) Not that we are sufficient of ourselves to think anything as of ourselves; but our sufficiency is of God;

(Phil 2:13 KJV) For it is God which worketh in you both to will and to do of his good pleasure.

(John 14:12 KJV) Verily, verily, I say unto you, He that believeth on me, the works that I do shall he do also; and greater works than these shall he do; because I go unto my Father.

(Phil 4:13 KJV) I can do all things through Christ which strengtheneth me.

(Luke 17:6 KJV) And the Lord said, If ye had faith as a grain of mustard seed, ye might say unto this sycamine tree, Be thou plucked up by the root, and be thou planted in the sea; and it should obey you.

(Mark 11:24 KJV) Therefore I say unto you, What things soever ye desire when ye pray, believe that ye receive them, and ye shall have them.

(2 Cor 2:14 KJV) Now thanks be unto God, which always causeth us to triumph in Christ, and maketh manifest the savour of his knowledge by us in every place.

(Phil 1:6 KJV) Being confident of this very thing, that he which hath begun a good work in you will perform it until the day of Jesus Christ:

(Phil 4:19 AMP) And my God will liberally supply (fill to the full) your every need according to His riches in glory in Christ Jesus.

(1 John 4:14 KJV) And we have seen and do testify that the Father sent the Son to be the Saviour of the world.

(Eph 6:11 KJV) Put on the whole armour of God that ye may be able to stand against the wiles of the devil.

(Mark 16:17 KJV) And these signs shall follow them that believe; in my name shall they cast out devils; they shall speak with new tongues;

(Rom 6:14 NIV) For sin shall not be your master, because you are not under law, but under grace.

(Luke 4:18 NIV) "The Spirit of the Lord is on me, because he has anointed me to preach good news to the poor. He has sent me to proclaim freedom for the prisoners and recovery of sight for the blind, to release the oppressed,

(Acts 1:8 NIV) But you will receive power when the Holy Spirit comes on you; and you will be my witnesses in Jerusalem, and in all Judea and Samaria, and to the ends of the earth."

(1 Cor 4:20 NIV) For the kingdom of God is not a matter of talk but of power.

(1 Cor 3:9 KJV) For we are labourers together with God: ye are God's husbandry, ye are God's building.

(2 Cor 5:20 KJV) Now then we are ambassadors for Christ, as though God did beseech you by us: we pray you in Christ's stead, be ye reconciled to God.

(Mark 16:15 KJV) And he said unto them, Go ye into all the world, and preach the gospel to every creature.

(Mat 16:19 KJV) And I will give unto thee the keys of the kingdom of heaven: and whatsoever thou shalt bind on earth shall be bound in heaven: and whatsoever thou shalt loose on earth shall be loosed in heaven.

(Luke 1:37 KJV) For with God nothing shall be impossible.

(2 Cor 2:14 NIV) But thanks be to God, who always leads us in triumphal procession in Christ and through us spreads everywhere the fragrance of the knowledge of him.

New Birth Blessing #9

As a new creature in Christ, I have a sound, clear mind. The Holy Spirit is my constant guide and teacher. As I yield to Him, my mind is transformed into the mind of Christ. Like Christ, my words now have creative abilities. I have what I speak. As I operate out of my recreated mind, the words that I speak, like Christ, are the words of my Father and His Word never returns to Him void or uncompleted.

(2 Tim 1:7 KJV) For God hath not given us the spirit of fear; but of power, and of love, and of a sound mind.

(Col 3:10 KJV) And have put on the new man, which is renewed in knowledge after the image of him that created him:

(Rom 12:2 KJV) And be not conformed to this world: but be ye transformed by the renewing of your mind, that ye may prove what is that good, and acceptable, and perfect, will of God.

(2 Cor 10:5 KJV) Casting down imaginations, and every high thing that exalteth itself against the knowledge of God, and bringing into captivity every thought to the obedience of Christ;

(Eph 4:23 KJV) And be renewed in the spirit of your mind;

(Col 2:10 KJV) And ye are complete in him, which is the head of all principality and power:

(1 Cor 2:16 KJV) For who hath known the mind of the Lord, that he may instruct him? But we have the mind of Christ.

(Eph 4:24 KJV) And that ye put on the new man, which after God is created in righteousness and true holiness.

(Col 3:16 KJV) Let the word of Christ dwell in you richly in all wisdom; teaching and admonishing one another in psalms and hymns and spiritual songs, singing with grace in your hearts to the Lord.

(1 Cor 2:12 KJV) Now we have received, not the spirit of word by the word of their testimony; they did not love their lives so much as to shrink from death.

(Mat 10:19-20 NIV)   But when they arrest you, do not worry about what to say or how to say it. At that time you will be given what to say, for it will not be you speaking, but the Spirit of your Father speaking through you.

(John 12:49-50 KJV) For I have not spoken of myself; but the Father which sent me, he gave me a commandment, what I should say, and what I should speak. And I know that his commandment is life everlasting: whatsoever I speak therefore, even as the Father said unto me, so I speak.

(Mat 18:19-20 KJV) Again I say unto you, that if two of you shall agree on earth as touching any thing that they shall ask, it shall be done for them of my Father which is in heaven. For where two or three are gathered together in my name, there am I in the midst of them.

(Mark 11:23-23 KJV)   For verily I say unto you, That whosoever shall say unto this mountain, Be thou removed, and be thou cast into the sea; and shall not doubt in his heart, but shall believe that those things which he saith shall come to pass; he shall have whatsoever he saith. Therefore I say unto you, What things soever ye desire, when ye pray, believe that ye receive them, and ye shall have them.

(Isa 55:11 KJV) So shall my word be that goeth forth out of my mouth: it shall not return unto me void, but it shall accomplish that which I please, and it shall prosper in the thing whereto I sent it.

New Birth Blessing #10

I'm not in competition with anyone for anything. My "getting" person has now become a "giving" person; I have the same kind of love for others that my Father has for me. We live to give!

(Rom 13:10 KJV) Love worketh no ill to his neighbour: therefore love is the fulfilling of the law.

(2 Cor 9:8 KJV) And God is able to make all grace abound toward you; that ye, always having all sufficiency in all things, may abound to every good work:

(Phil 4:19 KJV) But my God shall supply all your need according to his riches in glory by Christ Jesus.

(James 1:27 KJV) Pure religion and undefiled before God and the Father is this, To visit the fatherless and widows in their affliction, and to keep himself unspotted from the world.

(James 3:17 KJV) But the wisdom that is from above is first pure, then peaceable, gentle, and easy to be entreated, full of mercy and good fruits, without partiality, and without hypocrisy.

(1 John 4:18 KJV) There is no fear in love; but perfect love casteth out fear: because fear hath torment. He that feareth is not made perfect in love.

(1 John 4:19 KJV) We love him, because he first loved us.

(Heb 13:16 KJV) But to do good and to communicate forget not: for with such sacrifices God is well pleased.

(Mat 22:37 KJV) Jesus said unto him, Thou shalt love the Lord thy God with all thy heart, and with all thy soul, and with all thy mind.

(Luke 14:11 KJV) For whosoever exalteth himself shall be abased; and he that humbleth himself shall be exalted.

(Song. 6:3) I am my beloved's; and my beloved is mine

(Acts 2:28 KJV) Thou hast made known to me the ways of life; thou shalt make me full of joy with thy countenance.

(Mat 28:20 NIV) and teaching them to obey everything I have commanded you. And surely I am with you always, to the very end of the age."

(Heb 13:5 KJV) Let your conversation be without covetousness; and be content with such things as ye have: for he hath said, I will never leave thee, nor forsake thee.

(John 10:30 KJV) I and my Father are one.

(John 14:20 KJV) At that day ye shall know that I am in my Father, and ye in me, and I in you.

(Col 2:10 KJV) And ye are complete in him, which is the head of all principality and power:

(1 Cor 1:9 KJV) God is faithful, by whom ye were called unto the fellowship of his Son Jesus Christ our Lord.

(Rom 8:38-39 KJV) For I am persuaded, that neither death, nor life, nor angels, nor principalities, nor powers, nor things present, nor things to come, Nor height, nor depth, nor any other creature, shall be able to separate us from the love of God, which is in Christ Jesus our Lord.

(John 14:23 KJV) Jesus answered and said unto him, If a man love me, he will keep my words: and my Father will love him, and we will come unto him, and make our abode with him.

(John 15:11 KJV) These things have I spoken unto you, that my joy might remain in you, and that your joy might be full.

(1 Cor 3:23 KJV) And ye are Christ's; and Christ is God's.

(Mat 18:19-20 KJV) Again I say unto you, That if two of you shall agree on earth as touching any thing that they shall ask, it shall be done for them of my Father which is in heaven. For where two or three are gathered together in my name, there am I in the midst of them.

(1 Cor 2:12 KJV) Now we have received, not the spirit of the world, but the spirit which is of God; that we might know the things that are freely given to us of God.

(Rom 8:38-39 KJV) For I am persuaded, that neither death, nor life, nor angels, nor principalities, nor powers, nor things present, nor things to come, Nor height, nor depth, nor any other creature, shall be able to separate us from the love of God, which is in Christ Jesus our Lord.

(Rom 14:17 KJV) For the kingdom of God is not meat and drink; but righteousness, and peace, and joy in the Holy Ghost.

(1 Pet 1:8 KJV) Whom having not seen, ye love; in whom, though now ye see him not, yet believing, ye rejoice with joy unspeakable and full of glory:

(Acts 2:13 KJV) …These men are full of new wine.

(John 15:11 KJV) These things have I spoken unto you, that my joy might remain in you, and that your joy might be full.

(Neh 8:10 NIV) Nehemiah said, "Go and enjoy choice food and sweet drinks, and send some to those who have nothing prepared. This day is sacred to our Lord. Do not grieve, for the joy of the LORD is your strength."

(Psa 16:11 NIV) You have made known to me the path of life; you will fill me with joy in your presence, with eternal pleasures at your right hand.

(Psa 21:6 NIV) Surely you have granted him eternal blessings and made him glad with the joy of your presence.

(Psa 30:11 NIV) You turned my wailing into dancing; you removed my sackcloth and clothed me with joy,

(Psa 126:2 NIV) Our mouths were filled with laughter, our tongues with songs of joy. Then it was said among the nations, "The LORD has done great things for them."

(Isa 55:12 KJV) For ye shall go out with joy, and be led forth with peace: the mountains and the hills shall break forth before you into singing, and all the trees of the field shall clap their hands.

(John 16:24 NIV) Until now you have not asked for anything in my name. Ask and you will receive, and your joy will be complete.

(Rom 14:17 NIV) For the kingdom of God is not a matter of eating and drinking, but of righteousness, peace and joy in the Holy Spirit,

New Birth Blessing #11

The best part is His presence. I walk with Him and I talk with Him and He shares with me His thoughts and ways. He is closer and more real to me than anything my senses can comprehend. And I am secure. I belong to Him, and He belongs to me.

(Song. 6:3 KJV) I am my beloved's; and my beloved is mine

(Acts 2:28 KJV) Thou hast made known to me the ways of life; thou shalt make me full of joy with thy countenance.

(Mat 28:20 KJV) Teaching them to observe all things whatsoever I have commanded you: and, lo, I am with you alway, even unto the end of the world. Amen.

(Heb 13:5 KJV) Let your conversation be without covetousness; and be content with such things as ye have: for he hath said, I will never leave thee, nor forsake thee.

(John 10:30 KJV) I and my Father are one.

(John 14:20 KJV) At that day ye shall know that I am in my Father, and ye in me, and I in you.

(Col 2:10 KJV) And ye are complete in him, which is the head of all principality and power:

(1 Cor 1:9 KJV) God is faithful, by whom ye were called unto the fellowship of his Son Jesus Christ our Lord.

(Rom 8:38 KJV) For I am persuaded, that neither death, nor life, nor angels, nor principalities, nor powers, nor things present, nor things to come,

(Rom 8:39 KJV) Nor height, nor depth, nor any other creature, shall be able to separate us from the love of God, which is in Christ Jesus our Lord.

(John 14:23 KJV) Jesus answered and said unto him, If a man love me, he will keep my words: and my Father will love him, and we will come unto him, and make our abode with him.

(John 15:11 KJV) These things have I spoken unto you, that my joy might remain in you, and that your joy might be full.

(1 Cor 3:23 KJV) And ye are Christ's; and Christ is God's.

(Mat 18:19 KJV) Again I say unto you, That if two of you shall agree on earth as touching any thing that they shall ask, it shall be done for them of my Father which is in heaven.

(Mat 18:20 KJV) For where two or three are gathered together in my name, there am I in the midst of them.

(1 Cor 2:12 KJV) Now we have received, not the spirit of the world, but the spirit which is of God; that we might know the things that are freely given to us of God.

Another "eleven" New Birth Blessing—

Did I mention the

JOY?

(Rom 14:17 KJV) For the kingdom of God is not meat and drink; but righteousness, and peace, and joy in the Holy Ghost.

(1 Pet 1:8 KJV) Whom having not seen, ye love; in whom, though now ye see him not, yet believing, ye rejoice with joy unspeakable and full of glory:

(Acts 2:13 KJV) ...These men are full of new wine.

(Neh 8:10 KJV) Then he said unto them, Go your way, eat the fat, and drink the sweet, and send portions unto them for whom nothing is prepared: for this day is holy unto our Lord: neither be ye sorry; for the joy of the LORD is your strength.

(Psa 5:11 KJV) But let all those that put their trust in thee rejoice: let them ever shout for joy, because thou defendest them: let them also that love thy name be joyful in thee.

(Psa 16:11 KJV) Thou wilt show me the path of life: in thy presence is fulness of joy; at thy right hand there are pleasures for evermore.

(Psa 30:5 KJV) For his anger endureth but a moment; in his favour is life: weeping may endure for a night, but joy cometh in the morning.

(Psa 105:43 KJV) And he brought forth his people with joy, and his chosen with gladness:

(Psa 126:5 KJV) They that sow in tears shall reap in joy.

(Isa 12:3 KJV) Therefore with joy shall ye draw water out of the wells of salvation.

(Isa 35:10 KJV) And the ransomed of the LORD shall return,

and come to Zion with songs and everlasting joy upon their heads: they shall obtain joy and gladness, and sorrow and sighing shall flee away.

(Isa 51:3 KJV) For the LORD shall comfort Zion: he will comfort all her waste places; and he will make her wilderness like Eden, and her desert like the garden of the LORD; joy and gladness shall be found therein, thanksgiving, and the voice of melody.

(Isa 55:12 KJV) For ye shall go out with joy, and be led forth with peace: the mountains and the hills shall break forth before you into singing, and all the trees of the field shall clap their hands.

(Isa 61:3 KJV) To appoint unto them that mourn in Zion, to give unto them beauty for ashes, the oil of joy for mourning, the garment of praise for the spirit of heaviness; that they might be called trees of righteousness, the planting of the LORD, that he might be glorified.

(Isa 61:7 KJV) For your shame ye shall have double; and for confusion they shall rejoice in their portion: therefore in their land they shall possess the double: everlasting joy shall be unto them.

(Jer 15:16 KJV) Thy words were found, and I did eat them; and thy word was unto me the joy and rejoicing of mine heart: for I am called by thy name, O LORD God of hosts.

(Mat 2:10 KJV) When they saw the star, they rejoiced with exceeding great joy.

(John 15:11 KJV) These things have I spoken unto you, that my joy might remain in you, and that your joy might be full.

(John 16:24 KJV) Hitherto have ye asked nothing in my name: ask, and ye shall receive, that your joy may be full.

(Acts 13:52 KJV) And the disciples were filled with joy, and with the Holy Ghost.

(Rom 14:17 KJV) For the kingdom of God is not meat and drink; but righteousness, and peace, and joy in the Holy Ghost.

(Rom 15:13 KJV) Now the God of hope fill you with all joy and peace in believing, that ye may abound in hope, through the power of the Holy Ghost.

(Heb 12:2 KJV) Looking unto Jesus the author and finisher of our faith; who for the joy that was set before him endured the cross, despising the shame, and is set down at the right hand of the throne of God.

(Jude 1:24-25 KJV) Now unto him that is able to keep you from falling, and to present you faultless before the presence of his glory with exceeding joy, To the only wise God our Saviour, be glory and majesty, dominion and power, both now and for ever. Amen.

These things have I spoken unto you,

that my joy might remain in you,

and that your joy might be full.

(Jn 15:11)

On the twelfth day of Christness
My Lord, He gave to me

TWELVE MONTHS TO PRAISE HIM!

Altogether Mighty, Altogether Holy, Altogether Worthy
To receive praise, honor, and glory.
You framed the worlds with Your Word,
All Creation is Yours and Yours alone.

Out of You, Father, a river of love
Creating an image of Your beauty above,
All worlds, all heavens, all images fair,
Of man and of beasts and of birds of the air,
All nature, all days, all bowing in praise,
Calling you Father, and Master, and Ancient of Days.
To the Only One worthy, and the Only One true.
Our praise and our worship are only Your due,
Our hearts are so humbled, our lips are struck dumb,
We worship the Father, the Spirit, the Son.
In Your presence my Lord is such fullness of Joy!
In Your presence is Zoe and it's mine to enjoy!
But more than Your presents is the look of Your Face,
I'm lost in Your Love and Your Beauty and Grace.
I call You Daddy, and You call me son,
Yet Awesome and Fearful Your Presence to some.
Your justice demands all iniquity found,
And routed and scourged and eternally bound.
That all men would know you and bow at your throne
Through Jesus Messiah Who brings us all home.

For a child is born to us, a son is given to us. And the government will rest on his shoulders. These will be his royal titles: Wonderful Counselor, Mighty God, Everlasting Father, Prince of Peace. His ever expanding, peaceful government will never end. He will rule forever with fairness and justice from the throne of his ancestor David. The passionate commitment of the LORD Almighty will guarantee this! (Isa 9:6 –7 NLT)

Knowing that Christ being raised from the dead dieth no more; death hath no more dominion over him. For in that he died, he died unto sin once: but in that he liveth, he liveth unto God. Likewise reckon ye also yourselves to be dead indeed unto sin, but alive unto God through Jesus Christ our Lord (Rom 6:9-11 KJV).

Now unto him that is able to keep you from falling, and to present you faultless before the presence of his glory with exceeding joy, To the only wise God our Saviour, be glory and majesty, dominion and power, both now and forever. Amen (Jude 1:24-25 KJV).

And being found in fashion as a man, he humbled himself, and became obedient unto death, even the death of the cross. Wherefore God also hath highly exalted him, and given him a name which is above every name: That at the name of Jesus every knee should bow, of things in heaven, and things in earth, and things under the earth; And that every tongue should confess that Jesus Christ is Lord, to the glory of God the Father (Phil 2:8-11 KJV).

Twelve is the number that represents government, order, and authority. There are twelve months in a year giving order to our days. Both sons of Abraham, Ishmael and Jacob, each had twelve sons. These sons became the princes of nations of two separate and distinct cultures, the Gentile and the Jewish. In Christ, the Messiah, these two worlds become one. Jesus gathered twelve apostles to establish the government of His church. Twelve is a number that establishes kingdoms.

The Bible is all about the Kingdom of God. What appears in shadow in the Old Testament comes to the light of substance in the New Testament. Jesus demonstrates the power and the authority of the Kingdom throughout His earthly ministry. He challenges the values we assume will bring us success and favor with God. He teaches a new kind of love, the one that dies to self-desire in favor of blessing and service. He shows us with His own life as well as with His words, that the way of the Kingdom of God is fairly opposite to the ways of the kingdom of man.

The Old Testament leads us from the earth's perfect beginnings to the fall of man and his world. Then the Abrahamic covenant of faith brings new beginnings and the promise of a New Kingdom for a covenant people. When they finally arrive at the Promised Land, God's people are faced with adversity, persecution, and even slavery. But the promise of a future Kingdom remains, and believers continue to wait in faith for the promised Messiah who will deliver them.

Four hundred years of silence from heaven follows the final chapter of the Old Testament. "Zion" is only an image engraved on the hearts and imaginations of those who will believe in the promise in spite of what their senses tell them. The promise of Messiah and a "New Jerusalem" has still to be revealed.

Yet in all these Old Testament wanderings, we see a God who is not "out there," in a kingdom to come, but is a Father Who is very present and involved in the affairs of His children. Unlike the gods of the tribes who persistently persecute and challenge the Old Testament Hebrew believers, Yahweh/Jehovah manifests Himself in power through the words and actions of His prophets. He uses elements like fire, water, and wind to assure His own people that He hears their prayers and that He is faithful to His covenant. To the enemies of His children, He declares that He is Lord over all the heavens and the earth. The Old Testament builds our faith that God will establish His kingdom with men.

Still, the Kingdom of God remains a mystery. Yahweh tells Moses, and later, allows Solomon to build Him tabernacles so that He can dwell among His people. The one Moses built was a movable tent that gave direction and comfort to the wandering Jews. Solomon's temple, built in the same pattern, also housed the Ark of the Covenant. There, in both tabernacles, Jehovah dwelt in an inner room called the Holy of Holies.

Jehovah God could dwell among His people, but He had no real intimacy with them. No one could enter that Holy Place of His Presence except the high priest once a year, and even then, he entered at the peril of his own life. The high priest's function was to offer atonement for the sins of the people. There was no sharing, no personal relationship between Jehovah God and His children. God was establishing His kingdom on earth, but it was not yet a kingdom where His children could enjoy intimacy with Him. The Old Covenant seemed more like a stumbling stone than a door to peace and prosperity with God.

The Mosaic Covenant of laws which God gave to Moses was the school teacher who taught us that we all needed more than a set of rules. Having rules would not save us because we could not possibly obey all of them all of the time. We needed a Covenant that wasn't dependent on our actions but on our trust in God's actions on our behalf. The Abrahamic Covenant promised such a kingdom would come. Then, at the fullness of time, the promised Messiah/Savior arrived. He came not as a mighty king but as helpless baby, not as a powerful master, but as meek and lowly servant, not as forceful lion but as a merciful lamb. This surely couldn't be the beginning of the new kingdom believers were expecting!

Most of the Jews never saw what they had been looking for. They had assumed that they understood all the Old Testament prophesies. They expected that their Messiah would take them out of their current political and economic misery. Their understandings of the style of the power and government of God were according to their human standards.

Even when Jesus claimed to be their long promised Messiah, they could not receive Him because He did not act the way they thought the Messiah *should* act. Rather than exerting His power to control or to force His way, He was meek and gentle. He taught in the temple and in the field with love and compassion. He did not judge the wicked. He offered them living water, healing and forgiveness of their sin. He did not enforce or respect religious rules and regulations. His judgment only fell on those whose hearts were empty of love and full of hypocrisy and greed. Jesus' ministry did not applaud the powerful, the prosperous, or the religiously "correct."

The one thing that the disciples of Jesus and the religious Jews knew was that *they did not understand the kingdom of God at all!* Instead of celebrating good works and faithful abiding of the laws, Jesus favored simple faith. Instead of giving his approval to the more famous religious leaders, Jesus identified with the bruised and broken, the hungry and thirsty, the weak and estranged. He spent significant times with the people that were considered unworthy of love or favor, and openly condemned the religious hypocrites who had no love for the people. Jesus simply didn't fit the "mold" of a true Messiah. And the religious leaders wanted to put Him away and even kill Him for it.

Even today, Jesus kicks out the legs of the chairs we rest so confidently upon in our own spiritual complacency. The mystery of the Kingdom of God continues to this day. We are still trying to earn God's love and favor by our own good works. We applaud self-reliance, proving to God that we are strong and good in the power of our might. But that's not the kind of relationship He is seeking with us. He rewards faith and reliance upon Him for all our needs. He exalts the humble and hears the prayers of children.

In this day of "correctness" we pride ourselves on our own "churchianity" for favor and blessing from God. Is the meager offering of that poor woman so much more valuable to God than the thousands I give for missions? Does the Lord embrace the prayer of that lowlife biker tattooed from head to toe over my mature and well-versed words to Him? And look at that girl who just loves to sit and pray! Doesn't she realize that she would be more blessed lending a hand in the church program?

The Gospel challenges all the smug assumptions that give us confidence that we are upstanding citizens of God's kingdom. We see Jesus favoring those people we traditionally look down on—street people, crooks, whores, and even little kids over respectable church-going, upright, hard-working adults. We can only question in our simple minds why the *last* is *first* in His kingdom.

What Jesus shows us in His ministry is that we already *have* the love and favor of our Father, God. Our Father is not a bookkeeper-Santa Claus God who only rewards good works and great behavior. We don't have to "do" anything to earn the gift of Kingdom life. The Kingdom of God is the gift of God in His Son, Jesus Christ. It belongs to *everyone.* We can't earn it or get it by performing any religious act or ritual. The Kingdom has come and it is available to all who would seek Him. We can't earn it; all our striving is in vain!

The Kingdom of God is for every human being. Jesus

ransomed every person who ever lived. Everyone has been saved. Everyone has access to the Spirit of God and the Kingdom of God. The *only* thing that prevents anyone from enjoying the Kingdom of God is unbelief, rejecting Jesus as personal Lord and savior. He is the door, the only door into this Kingdom, and the only key that opens that door is faith, the kind of heart agreement that makes us "*Christed.*"

Jesus brought the revelation that the Kingdom is founded on relationship in love of the "losing" kind. He demonstrated that love by doing things we have so much trouble accepting—things like never closing the door of His heart to us. In fact, He even forgets our offenses and sin, and never holds our past against us. He took our real guilt and made it His to justify and acquit us.

He then went on to recreate and restore us to Himself in a relationship of love and faith, not requiring anything else from us. He brought us back into our Kingdom inheritance as Sons and Daughters of Abba Father God, with the intimacy that our ancestors, Adam and Eve, had forfeited in their treason against God. What's more, He did not leave us alone. He sent the Holy Spirit to teach, comfort, and empower us. He even sends angels, His messengers, to aid and protect us! All we can do is to get "lost" in that kind of love to know His kingdom! Losing our life, we will find it (Matt 10:39).

The Kingdom of God challenges our traditional worldly concepts of winning and losing. Winners in this kingdom are the ones who admit their utter inability to make themselves right with God. Winners are the ones who totally depend, rely upon and trust God to lead, guide, protect, comfort, and care for every their every need. Winners' good works are simply an overflow of the love and the grace they have received from God. They don't have to *do* anything or perform to earn admittance or merit in this Kingdom.

These winners are the salt in the soup of day-to-day living; they are the light that gives comfort, warmth, and revelation to a hungry people. They are the hands that make the load lighter, the feet that go that extra mile to bless another, the ambassadors that bring peace, hope, and good will to an alien culture. In the Kingdom of God, the humble are exalted, the last are first, the greatest are the servants, and that those who lose their lives find them.

Jesus came to declare that the Kingdom of God is also *here* in the eternal *now*, on this earth. It is a spiritual reality that the kingdom of man cannot know. The Kingdom of God contains no corruption (1 Cor 15:50). And neither can God's children bring any corruption into this Kingdom. How is that possible? Only one way—the blood of Jesus cleanses us of all corruption and that is the way we enter and remain in the Kingdom of God (John 3:3). It's open to everyone who will submit to the way.   This lifestyle honors repentance and heart-faith in a continual walk with the Lord Jesus. This lifestyle commands dependence and reliance on God alone. Only unbelief can keep a person from enjoying the love, the life, the mercy, the protection, and the power of the Kingdom of God. Faith is the currency that makes us rich.

The Bible says this kingdom exists in the Holy Spirit

(Rom 14:17). Everything that He is and does manifests the Kingdom of God. What's it like? Can we guess? Well, yes, in part we can. But it will take our lifetime here and in eternity to comprehend it and know it fully!

The Father has declared His Son Jesus Christ the King of this Kingdom as well as of all others. The office of government rests upon His shoulders now and forever.(Isa 9:6-7). King of Kings and Lord of Lords, Jesus is our very approachable, compassionate, Lamb of God who identified with us so that we could find ourselves in Him. He is also the awesome, incomparable Holy, Righteous, and Just Lion of Judah. The Word declares that every knee shall bow and every tongue shall confess that Jesus Christ is Lord of all, in heaven, on earth, and under the earth (Phil 2:9-11). It is His Kingdom.

The Kingdom of God is the true, eternal reality. It has always existed in the heart of the Father, and God is establishing it now on earth one heart at a time. The Word tells us that the Kingdom is within (Lk 17:22). It is as simple as peace and as complex as power. It is peace that the world can't give or take away. It's the inner knower that you and God make a majority, and that He is in control so you don't have to be. It's power to create, to establish, and to abide in His Word here and now (1 Cor 4:20). It's the power that heals the sick and the brokenhearted, brings hope and faith to hurting hearts, and breaks the chains of destructive habit patterns that try to rule our lives (Lk 4:18-19). It's the power that enforces the Word of God in our hearts and in the lives of others. It's the power to live like Jesus and love like Jesus. It's the power of the *Christed* life.

The Kingdom of God abides now in our hearts. And it's also a kingdom coming, for we only see in part now what will be ours when Christ returns. The Beatitudes give us an outline of the government of this Kingdom. The Laws or Principles that absolutely rule this Kingdom are created to bless its citizens abundantly! It is motivated by love of the giving kind, which assumes no expectation of return or reward. Jesus says it's a priceless treasure.

The Kingdom is dynamic. Like dynamite it explodes with power that changes things we could not change on our own. Time does not heal the experiences of rejection, betrayal, abandonment, hurtful words, abuse, and all the offenses that bruise our hearts. Time simply hardens our hearts. We need Kingdom power to become whole.

Jesus showed us the way. Even on the cross, He prayed, "Father, forgive them, for they know not what they do." Forgiveness removes the power that bruises, binds, and barrages our hearts. Forgiveness allows the festered wounds we protect so carefully, and, so inadequately, to be healed. Forgiveness removes the trigger from the gun that attacks the unhealed wounds of our lives. So the evil that would bind and bruise us cannot even touch our hearts.

This is the Kingdom lifestyle that "restores our souls." The offenses, the hurts, the attacks, the "tares of our heart" that come from others, Jesus says by comparison, should not be dealt with by attacking the one who wounded us, but by forgiving him! Forgiveness is the secret to freedom of heart. It is a dynamic, life-empowering Kingdom principle.

The Kingdom of God is alive in us and through us. As the children of the King, abiding in the Kingdom of God, we have received delegated authority along with the power of the Holy Spirit to back it up. That means that we do not have to live as victims or slaves of evils that once captivated and ruled our lives (John 8:36).

The Kingdom of God is a kingdom of God's unconditional love. It is a love that will not let us go, but will seek us, woo us, wash us, lift us, engulf us, comfort us, and just bless us beyond our ability to ask, think, or even imagine (1 Cor 2:9). It is a free gift, this wonderful mystery of the love of God.

The best thing we can do to enjoy the Kingdom of God is to hear the Word, accept it, and allow it to bear fruit in our lives. The less we interfere by "helping God" or by "earning His favor," the greater will be our benefits. My personal prayer has become, "Lord, don't let me block the view!" and "Help me to keep my hands off *Your* work!"

When we are born again, recreated in the God-class, we have the privilege of the abiding presence of God in our everyday lives. That means that the kingdom of God is *in us* operating by the power of God Himself. As He transforms us, our lives will bear fruit that will expand the kingdom not only in our own hearts, but also in the hearts of others.

This is the way the Kingdom multiplies. Our own transformations are the light and the love that Christ uses to woo and win those who are hungry and thirsty for new life. We are the "Jesus with skin on" that will bring hope and healing to the wounded and lost.

The Kingdom of God is a community of "living stones" fit together perfectly by the Holy Spirit to form a temple, a city, a kingdom for God to dwell in and operate from. He no longer has to live in a tent or a concrete building, but now He has established abiding intimacy with each and every one of His children. Each "stone" is individually precious, a true treasure to God. And as a body, a building, a "temple" or "city," those stones are corporately powerful, transcending every other kingdom on or under the earth. With Christ as the head, the "greater works" can come forth in us and through us (Jn 14:12).

The Father's heart is that we, His children, be whole and perfect (Matt 5:48; Rom 12:2). We are judged only by what Jesus did for us on the cross. Jesus came to that end. The kingdom of God has been at work in this world since the creation. By His death and resurrection, Christ reconciled everything, on earth and in heaven, to Himself. Most importantly, He reconciled you and me to our Father. He recreated us, and gave us an altogether new life, a new name, and a new identity, a new family, a new community, complete with awesome power and authority. Most importantly, He gave our lives meaning and purpose, and He gave us His heart to love and enjoy for all eternity.

At the end, He makes all things new—earth and heaven. The Bible explains that the "New Jerusalem" is the very real Kingdom of God in its full manifestation. We are a part of it, and in this eternal kingdom, which began before the foundations of the earth, we shall lack nothing; nor shall we ever come to an end of the wonder of it all.

There is only one response we can offer to the One whose love has given us this incredible life. There is only one response to the One who reconciled us to our Father, who recreated us in His own nature, who gave us His name and His very life. The kingdom He promised began in us the moment we said, "yes" to Jesus, and it will continue and only get better! There is only one true response.

As we bow before His throne, as we dance the dance of life in His arms, as we rest peacefully upon His breast, as we rejoice in jubilant abandon in His presence, as we weep with tears of sorrow for sin and unbelief, as we shout with a voice of triumph, as we lie prostrate humbly before Him, as we rise and as we lie down, as we come and as we go, in whatever state we find ourselves in, there is only one response—to praise and worship Him always.

With our whole heart, with our whole mind, and with our whole lives, now and through eternity in the kingdom of God we shall sing His praise and worship His Name forever. Together with all the hosts of heaven, and the entire kingdom of God, we shall praise the Lord God which is His due.

> And the four beasts had each of them six wings about *him*; and *they were* full of eyes within: and they rest not day and night, saying, Holy, holy, holy, Lord God Almighty, which was, and is, and is to come. And when those beasts give glory and honor and thanks to him that sat on the throne, who liveth forever and ever, The four and twenty elders fall down before him that sat on the throne, and worship him that liveth forever and ever, and cast their crowns before the throne, saying, Thou art worthy, O Lord, to receive glory and honor and power: for thou hast created all things, and for thy

pleasure they are and were created.

(Rev 4:8-11 KJV)

What better befits a *Christed* life? What better befits our awesome and wonderful Father, our precious and marvelous Lord, Jesus Christ, and our sensitive and loving Holy Spirit?

"Praise God from whom all blessings flow, praise Him all creatures, here below; praise Him above, ye heavenly host; praise Father, Son, and Holy Ghost." (Traditional doxology)

RELATED SCRIPTURES (KJV)

Psa 8:4-6 What is man, that thou art mindful of him? and the son of man, that thou visitest him? For thou hast made him a little lower than the angels, and hast crowned him with glory and honour. Thou madest him to have dominion over the works of thy hands: thou hast put all things under his feet:

Psa 145:10-14 All thy works shall praise thee, O LORD; and thy saints shall bless thee. They shall speak of the glory of thy kingdom, and talk of thy power; To make known to the sons of men his mighty acts, and the glorious majesty of his kingdom. Thy kingdom is an everlasting kingdom, and thy dominion endureth throughout all generations. The LORD upholdeth all that fall, and raiseth up all those that be bowed down.

Rom 6:14 For sin shall not have dominion over you: for ye are not under the law, but under grace.

Mat 6:33 But seek ye first the kingdom of God, and his righteousness: and all these things shall be added unto you.

Mat 12:28 But if I cast out devils by the Spirit of God, then the kingdom of God is come unto you.

Mark 4:30–32 And he said, Whereunto shall we liken the kingdom of God? or with what comparison shall we compare it? It is like a grain of mustard seed, which, when it is sown in the earth, is less than all the seeds that be in the earth: But when it is sown, it groweth up, and becometh greater than all herbs, and shooteth out great branches; so that the fowls of the air may lodge under the shadow of it.

Mark 10:14-15 But when Jesus saw it, he was much displeased, and said unto them, Suffer the little children to come unto me, and forbid them not: for of such is the kingdom of God. Verily I say unto you, Whosoever shall not receive the kingdom of God as a little child, he shall not enter therein.

Luke 4:43   And he said unto them, I must preach the kingdom of God to other cities also: for therefore am I sent.

Luke 7:28   For I say unto you, Among those that are born of women there is not a greater prophet than John the Baptist: but he that is least in the kingdom of God is greater than he.

Luke 9:2   And he sent them to preach the kingdom of God, and to heal the sick.

Luke 9:11   And the people, when they knew it, followed him: and he received them, and spake unto them of the kingdom of God, and healed them that had need of healing.

Luke 9:62   And Jesus said unto him, No man, having put his hand to the plow, and looking back, is fit for the kingdom of God.

Luke 10:9 And heal the sick that are therein, and say unto them, The kingdom of God is come nigh unto you.

Luke 12:31   But rather seek ye the kingdom of God; and all these things shall be added unto you.

Luke 13:29-30 And they shall come from the east, and from the west, and from the north, and from the south, and shall sit down in the kingdom of God. And, behold, there are last which shall be first, and there are first which shall be last.

Luke 16:16 The law and the prophets were until John: since that time the kingdom of God is preached, and every man presseth into it.

Luke 17:20-21   And when he was demanded of the Pharisees, when the kingdom of God should come, he answered them and said, the kingdom of God cometh not with observation: Neither shall they say, Lo here! or, lo there! for, behold, the kingdom of God is within you.

Luke 19:11   And as they heard these things, he added and spake a parable, because he was nigh to Jerusalem, and because they thought that the kingdom of God should immediately appear.

John 3:5 Jesus answered, Verily, verily, I say unto thee, except a man be born of water and of the Spirit, he cannot enter into the kingdom of God.

Acts 1:3   To whom also he showed himself alive after his passion by many infallible proofs, being seen of them forty days, and speaking of the things pertaining to the kingdom of God:

Rom 14:7 For none of us liveth to himself, and no man dieth to himself.

1 Cor 4:20   For the kingdom of God is not in word, but in power.

1 Cor 15:15   Yea, and we are found false witnesses of God; because we have testified of God that he raised up Christ: whom he raised not up, if so be that the dead rise not.

Phil 4:6 Be careful for nothing; but in every thing by prayer and supplication with thanksgiving let your requests be made known unto God.

PRAYER OF FAITH

FATHER, THANK YOU
FOR GIVING ME A SAVIOR,
REDEEMER, KINSMAN, BROTHER, LORD—JESUS
THANK YOU FOR RECREATING IN ME THE
SUPERNATURAL IDENTITY THAT SIN STOLE.
THANK YOU FOR THE LIVING WORD IN WHOM
I LIVE AND MOVE AND HAVE MY LIFE.
THANK YOU FOR YOUR PRECIOUS PROMISES THAT ARE
FOR ME NOW AND FOREVERMORE.
THANK YOU FOR THE WORD OF FAITH THAT IS
ON MY LIPS AND IN MY HEART.
THANK YOU FOR GIVING ME A DIVINE DESTINY
THAT YOU HAVE EQUIPPED ME TO FULFILL.
THANK YOU FOR THE PEACE THAT LEADS ME AND KEEPS
ME IN YOUR PERFECT REST.
THANK YOU FOR THE JOY THAT IS
MY STRENGTH AND MY SONG.
THANK YOU FOR THE INIMACY THAT WE SHARE.
AND THANK YOU FOR THE HOLY SPIRIT
WHO ABIDES IN MY HEART AND EMPOWERS ME
WITH THE SAME ANOINTING THAT MY LORD
JESUS CHRIST MANIFESTED IN HIS EARTHLY MINISTRY.
THANK YOU FOR MAKING ME A
NEW CREATION,
YOUR OWN CHILD,
YOUR BELOVED,
THE APPLE OF
YOUR EYE.
I RECEIVE
I BELIEVE
I TRUST YOU
I RELY ON YOU
I REST IN FAITH
ASSURED OF THE OUTCOME.

What shall separate us
from the love of Christ?
Shall tribulation, or distress,
or persecution, or famine,
or nakedness, or peril, or sword?
As it is written, For thy sake we are killed all the day
long; we are accounted as sheep for the slaughter. Nay,
in all these things we are more than conquerors through
him that loved us.
For I am persuaded,
that neither death,
nor life, nor angels,
nor principalities, nor powers,
nor things present,
nor things to come,
nor height, nor depth,
nor any other creature,
shall be able to separate us
from the love of God,
which is in Christ Jesus our Lord.

(Rom 8:35-39 KJV)

ENDNOTES

[1] *Oxford American Dictionary,* Oxford University Press, New York (1980) vs. "heart"

[2] Reinhard Bonnke, *Mighty Manifestations.* Creation House, Lake Mary, FL (1994), pg. 9.

[3] Rodney Howard-Browne, *The Touch of God.* Revival Ministries International, Tampa, FL (1992), pg. 50

[4] Heflin, Ruth Ward, *Revival Glory.* McDougal Publishing, Hagerstown, MD, (1998), pg 65.

[5] Finis Jennings Dake, *Dake's Annotated Reference Bible.* Lawrenceville, GA 30246 p. 314

[6] ibid.

[7] Barbara Stephens, *Solutions.* Abundant Life Ministries, Pensacola, FL (2007) pg. 2.

[8] Edward Chumney, *The Seven Festivals of the Messiah.* Destiny Image Publishers, PA, (1999), pg. 95-131.

BIBLIOGRAPHY

Bonnke, Reinhard, Mighty *Manifestations*. Creation House, Lake Mary, FL (1994).

Capon, Robert Farrar, *The Parables of the Kingdom*. William B. Eerdmans Publishing Co., Grand Rapids, MI (1985).

Chumney, Edward, *The Seven Festivals of the Messiah*. Destiny Image Publishers, Shippensburg, PA (1994).

Clark, Randy, *There is More*. Global Awakening, Mechanicsburg, PA (2005).

Dake, Finis Jennings, Dake's *Annotated Reference Bible*. Dake Bible Sales, Inc., Lawrenceville, GA (1989)

Dunn, Benjamin, *The Happy Gospel*. Destiny Image Publishers, Shippensburg, PA (2011).

Ehrlich, Eugene, et. al. *Oxford American Dictionary*, Oxford University Press, New York (1980).

Heflin, Ruth Ward, *Revival Glory*. McDougal Publishers, Hagerstown, MD (1998).

Howard-Browne, Rodney, *The Touch of God*. Revival Ministries International, Tampa FL (1992).

Johnson, Bill, *The Supernatural Power of a Transformed Mind*. Destiny Image Publishers, Shippensburg, PA (2005).

Pickett, Fuchsia, Receiving *Divine Revelation*. Creation House, Orlando, FL (1997).

Stephens, Barbara, Solutions. Abundant Life Ministries, Pensacola, FL (2002).

Strong, James. *The New Strong's Exhaustive Concordance of the Bible*. Thomas Nelson Publishers, Nashville, TN (1990).

CPSIA information can be obtained at www.ICGtesting.com
Printed in the USA
BVOW02s0721050716

454187BV00005B/11/P